GENESIS

ENDGAME TRILOGY

GENESIS

BOOK ONE OF THE ENDGAME TRILOGY

JEFF ACKENBACK

iUniverse LLC
Bloomington

GENESIS
Book One of the Endgame Trilogy

iUniverse books may be ordered through booksellers or by contacting:

iUniverse LLC
1663 Liberty Drive
Bloomington, IN 47403
www.iuniverse.com
1-800-Authors (1-800-288-4677)

ISBN: 978-1-4917-0292-5 (sc)
ISBN: 978-1-4917-0294-9 (hc)
ISBN: 978-1-4917-0293-2 (ebk)

Library of Congress Control Number: 2013915047

Printed in the United States of America

iUniverse rev. date: 08/20/2013

CHAPTER 1

DANTE

As a child, Dante Smith had dreamed of doing something with his life that would have made his father proud. Since losing his father to an unexplained workplace accident just after Dante's fourth birthday, he'd done everything he could to live up to his father's reputation. Conner Smith had been, among other things, a father and husband first, an astronaut second. Whenever someone who had known Conner would meet Dante for the first time, they would inevitably comment on the strong resemblance he bore to his father. Though Dante stood a few inches taller, he carried his 6'3" frame in nearly the exact same way his father had. Dante had considered growing a full beard like his father had done near the end of his life. At the time, Dante had simply seen his father as superhuman, an almost mythical figure, and it was only through old pictures that he'd realized there were touches of gray peppered into Conner's otherwise raven-black hair and beard. Anytime Dante attempted to go past his traditional goatee, though, his wife or someone he worked with would make a "helpful" comment, and Dante would give in and stick to what he knew worked.

"Hey! Watch where you're walking . . ." someone yelled from their car, the sound of their blaring horn blocking out whatever followed and shaking Dante's thoughts back to the present.

Dante laughed to himself and politely waved, taking a step back from the cross walk and straightening his bright red tie, which at the moment matched the tone of his face. He hated wearing suits, especially on days when he would choose to walk to work, simply because they never felt right on him. Taking a moment to gather himself and refocus on his path home, Dante checked his watch, then removed his black suit jacket, folding it up and sticking it in his briefcase. He knew that such a move would end up haunting him once he finally made it home, but the warm Miami weather had finally caught up to him, with a couple of blocks still left on his trek. No one in Dante's life understood why he would walk several miles through the city and into the suburbs, when driving would cut off roughly an hour from the commute. Most of the time, Dante chose not to explain it, as most people would stick to their opinions regardless. On the rare occasions when he felt like having a longer conversation about it, Dante would simply state that the long walk gave him necessary time to transition from his work life to his home life. While that was true for the most part, Dante always kept his main reason to himself: he just felt better when he was in open space, unconfined and able to physically control his journey.

With no further incidents, Dante finally made his way home. His house was nothing special, but it was still the largest and nicest in which he'd ever lived. When his father had died, his life insurance had been more than enough to take care of Dante and his mother. Even in the weeks just after Conner's death, Becky had done her best to educate Dante on the wisdom of properly investing. It had paid off for both of them, as the life insurance money and pension had continued to grow and provide nearly an unlimited income, though Dante always suspected that someone else had been watching out for them somehow. Dante had known that Becky Smith, his mother, had taken Conner's death hard, but she'd never lost faith, in herself or her beliefs. She continued to read the Bible every night and go to church every time the doors were open, even though Dante had stopped going in college. It wasn't that he necessarily had rebelled against the ideals and belief system of the church, but he just found that he had less and less time. It was the one thing about his life that Dante knew somewhat disappointed his mother, and it was always his intention to at least superficially get back into church attendance.

Seeing that Gwen's car was home, Dante shook away any remaining thoughts of his past and straightened his suit. They'd been married for three years, but he still felt a desire to impress her each time he entered the home. Dante quickly checked his briefcase, making sure that it was the one adorned with the company logo, then calmly and confidently walked through the door. Dante could hear the upstairs shower running, so he sighed and placed his briefcase by the door, removing his suit coat but keeping his tie in place. All of the rooms downstairs were still dark, which meant that Gwen had most likely had a rough day. Though he knew his job was quite difficult, Dante couldn't imagine why or how someone could spend all day teaching high school, much less high school

English, which was routinely butchered more and more each day by the students. Whenever Dante would ask Gwen why she chose to live her life assigning and grading seemingly pointless essays and stories, she would simply look at him and smile and say, "I suppose it's better than doing taxes." Firmly put in his place, Dante would always feign hurt and pout for a few minutes. Dante had graduated Princeton at the top of his class with degrees in biochemistry and political science, so his life definitely wasn't how he'd once pictured it, but as he heard Gwen making her way down the stairs and his heart began beating faster, he knew it was still a life that he wanted.

"Dante? Did I hear you come in finally?" Gwen asked.

In a strangely light-hearted mood, Dante leaned his head back in the chair, pretending to be asleep. He subtly peeked out of the corner of his eye as Gwen walked into the room, still drying her hair. Unable to control his smile at seeing his wife, Dante let out a small cough, hoping that it would do the job of covering it up. As Gwen stood in front of him, arms crossed and cleared her throat, Dante stretched his arms and rapidly blinked his eyes. He looked around the room, doing his best to act as if he'd been there for quite a while. From time to time, Dante would allow himself to act foolishly or even appear to be comic relief, usually just to make Gwen smile. When she would smile, Dante's entire room would seem to brighten. He loved seeing the way her piercing blue eyes would almost dance in the light when she smiled, her long, blonde hair cascading off her shoulders and providing a stark contrast to her porcelain skin. At 5'7" she was considered tall for a woman, but since Dante still towered above her, he would often call her "shorty," simply because no one else had. Seeing that his playacting had not had the desired effect, Dante smiled and stood, hugging Gwen tightly and kissing her on the forehead.

"Bad day?" Dante asked, still holding her.

"Just a long day," Gwen replied, resting her head on Dante's chest. "I had to undo some of the damage the last sub did. She decided, on her own mind you, that throwing out the words 'APA format' would be enough to teach . . . nevermind, I don't want to talk about it. How was your day?"

"It was . . . a normal day," Dante replied, taking a step back and releasing the hug. "You know how it is . . . carry the one, add column B . . . a monkey could do it, as long as that monkey is incredibly smart, dedicated and has a calculator."

"You know you don't have to be stuck there," Gwen said. "You've got degrees in . . ."

"Yeah, I know, but what I do . . . well, it has to be done. Want to go out for dinner?" Dante said, hoping to change the subject.

"Only if we can go somewhere that will accept me looking like a homeless person in these sweats," Gwen replied.

"If all homeless people look like you now, then there's going to be a major increase in men working at shelters," Dante said.

Dante leaned down and kissed Gwen softly on the lips, making a mental note to once again call John Dawson, his mentor, and thank him for setting them up on a blind date five years ago. Before Dante had a chance to follow up with another compliment, though, he caught sight of a dark red stain on his left sleeve. After taking off his coat, he'd immediately gone to the chair to pretend to be asleep, so the rather small yet important detail had eluded his attention. Dante knew that if he was too obvious in hiding his sleeve now, Gwen would immediately notice. Instead, he gently hugged her again and then turned towards the stairs to quickly change his clothes. As he rounded the corner and began heading up the steps, he could hear Gwen humming behind him, moving things around and keeping herself busy. Breathing a sigh of relief, Dante grabbed a pair of shorts and a t-shirt and headed into the bathroom to shower.

Shutting but not locking the door behind him, Dante turned on the shower, then took off his shirt and ran hot water from the sink onto the sleeve, scrubbing it as hard as he could. Rubbing soap onto it, Dante realized that he was only succeeding in making the stain larger, though the dark red had lightened some at least. Still scrubbing, Dante looked in the mirror, wincing at the black circles under his eyes. He was only 25, yet he felt as if he looked at least a decade older. As wonderful and wholesome as his home life was, his professional life was beginning to catch up with him. Unfortunately, though, he could see no way to reconcile that, at least not without a much better reason than "I've been tired and stressed lately." Gwen was right, that Dante had spent too much time working on his dual majors to be stuck in a job doing something he didn't love, but she only knew half of the story. Though she was speaking from a place of love, Dante knew she had no idea who he really was or what he really did, and he honestly wasn't sure how she would take it if she did.

⋆ ⋆ ⋆

CHAPTER 2

GWEN

GWEN HAD NEVER BEEN THE girl that had dreamed about a man coming along to sweep her off her feet and marry her. She'd never had illusions that marriage would be a fairy tale, perfect and always happy, nor did she believe that whatever man she would end up with would be Prince Charming. She did, however, hold herself to certain standards. She'd dated off and on through high school, but once she'd gone to college, she'd decided to only date someone that fit all her criteria for a good husband. It wasn't that she was hoping to marry early or always had it on her mind, just that she had seen far too many of her friends lower themselves to date a certain type of guy, then allow themselves to be stuck in marriages that simply didn't work. When Gwen had first met Dante, she'd already learned a great deal about him and his character through her uncle John. One of her biggest requirements had been honesty, and Dante had always given her that in spades. Until today, that is.

Gwen busied herself, humming and idly moving things around, waiting for Dante to take his shower. She'd noticed the dark red stain on his shirt almost immediately, though she'd given him the benefit of the doubt and waited for his explanation, which had never arrived. Whereas many women would jump to the conclusion that their husband was cheating on them, Gwen felt reasonably confident that Dante was as faithful as he was honest, which meant that the reason for the stain had to be something serious enough for him to conceal it, though not involving another woman. As she straightened the wedding picture which adorned the living room wall, Gwen tried to convince herself that she was overreacting, that it was just a food stain and nothing that even warranted an explanation. She had a feeling, though, an awful feeling in her gut that wouldn't go away, and so she knew she needed to see it for herself.

As Gwen walked up the stairs and through the bedroom she and Dante shared into the master bath, she felt a mixture of guilt and fear.

She trusted Dante, and throughout the entire time she'd known him, he'd never given her cause to doubt anything about him. However, something about the stain just didn't set right with her, and she was resolute in finding out whether it was something or nothing. If it was just a food stain, then she'd laugh and explain everything to Dante right there in the bathroom. No matter how hard she tried to imagine various things it could be, though, she truly had no idea what it was about it that worried her. Seeing the steam rise out from behind the curtain and hearing Dante softly singing to himself, Gwen knew that her time was limited. Dante had never been one to "waste time standing up in the shower," as he put it, so she quietly and quickly walked into the bathroom and did a scan for the shirt. Her heart stopped momentarily when she saw it half-soaking, half-hanging out of the sink. If Dante had thought to attempt to get rid of the stain, then, regardless of whether or not she knew why, her reasons to be concerned were validated.

With a feeling of dread washing over her, Gwen prayed for the courage to simply call out to Dante and end the charade right there. She had no doubts that he was faithful, so the stain couldn't be lipstick. He wasn't a violent man, so the odds were strongly against it being someone else's blood. It was with that thought that Gwen realized what was bothering her so much. She'd been partially raised by her uncle John Dawson, a well decorated, lifelong military man, so she'd dealt with her share of worrying about someone's physical wellbeing. Since Dante was an accountant, there was little chance he'd been injured at work, at least not without it being quarterly tax time. If the stain was blood, and Gwen felt a sureness that it was, then it would probably be Dante's. If he was attempting to cover it up, as it appeared that he was, then it was probable that he didn't want her to know something was physically wrong with him. The placement of the stain would make it approximately the right spot for Dante to have coughed up blood.

Realizing that she was driving herself insane, Gwen shook the nonsense out of her head and quietly sighed to herself, gathering up her resolve. She reached into the sink and carefully lifted up the sleeve, holding it close to her nose, first, then her eyes. Though it was partially washed out, Gwen was positive it was blood. With her worst fears possibly confirmed, Gwen slowly walked back out of the bathroom and sat down on the bed. She had no idea how long she'd been sitting there when Dante walked out of the bathroom drying his shaggy, black hair and whistling some tune that she may have recognized if her thoughts weren't miles away. The sound of the phone in the distance slightly brought her out of her daze, and, realizing that Dante was now looking at her, she put on a fake half-smile and acted as if her mind wasn't forcing her to go through every negative possibility for Dante hiding a blood stain from her. She'd never been particularly jealous or distrusting or worrisome, so she had no idea what it was about this particular event that was causing her to bypass her normal behavior and simply talk to her husband. There was something dreadful about the whole thing, and, if Dante had asked her what was wrong, she wasn't quite sure she would be able to even put it into words.

"Gwen? That's my cell, could you come back from wherever you are and get it for me while I change?" Dante said, heading back into the bathroom.

"Of course, I'll . . ." Gwen picked up the phone, not bothering to finish her sentence. "Hello?"

"I'm having trouble with my cable service, could you send someone out?" a deep, masculine voice boomed through the phone.

"I'm . . . I'm sorry?" Gwen said, the absurdity of the call bringing her back to her senses. "You must have the wrong number . . ."

Before Gwen had a chance to ask what number the person had meant to dial, the call was cut off from the other end. Gwen looked at the phone for a moment, smiling to herself at the phone's wallpaper, which was a picture of Spider-Man, something she knew a picture of her could never compete with for her husband, at least when it came to his phone. The childlike innocence of the picture combined with the fact that Dante had asked her to answer his phone without even pausing told Gwen that she had to be wrong about everything she'd assumed about the stain. She wasn't married to the type of man that would hide things and lie about them, but rather the type of man that trusted and loved her completely. Gwen set the phone down and walked into the bathroom, hugging her half-dressed husband from behind, leaning her face against his still-damp back.

"Who was it, babe?" Dante said, turning around and returning the hug. "Everything okay?"

"Wrong number, something about cable," Gwen said. "You think that's funny, wait until I tell you what I've . . ."

"I just realized I forgot to lock my office door," Dante said, his body tensing and pulling away from Gwen's embrace. "I need to run back into work and take care of that before something gets stolen."

"What could possibly be stolen from an accountant's office?" Gwen asked. "Besides, I'm sure the building is locked down."

"I'm really sorry, Gwen. I've . . . I'll get chewed out if I mess this up one more time," Dante said, pulling on a shirt and swiftly leaving the bathroom. "I'll be back as soon as I can . . ."

"I'll just come with you. Then we can grab something to eat from downtown," Gwen said, following him and feeling the sense of dread return.

By the time she made it out of the bathroom, only seconds behind Dante, he'd already slipped on his pants and socks and had almost finished tying his shoes.

"Since I'll already be there, I'll just go ahead and knock out some of tomorrow's work, so we can have a full-fledged date tomorrow night instead," Dante said, standing up and kissing Gwen quickly. "I know this seems weird, but . . . well, I'll explain it later. I'm really sorry, Gwen. I promise, I'll make it up to you."

Gwen stood silently, watching as Dante raced out the bedroom door. She could hear his hurried pace as he bounded down the stairs, then slammed the front door. The sound of the engine roared through the otherwise quiet night, and Gwen knew that somehow, some way, everything that had just happened was tied together. Throughout her life before Dante, there had only been one person she'd really felt as if she could count on when she needed help, and for some reason she couldn't quite put her finger on, she felt that need right then. Gwen slowly walked over to the dresser and picked up her cell phone, looking half-aware through the contacts, until she got to the name she was seeking. The phone only rang for a moment before the other end picked up. Gwen didn't wait for the greeting.

"John? I need you," Gwen said. "I'm worried about Dante."

* * *

CHAPTER 3

JOHN

John Dawson had spent nearly his entire life in the service of his country, and it was one of the two accomplishments in his life for which he allowed himself to feel great pride. As Gwendolyn Watson's uncle, John had found the fulfillment of family which he'd always felt had been denied to him. Though his relationship with his sister, Gwendolyn's mother, had never truly been able to overcome its obstacles, John had managed to play a large role in Gwendolyn's life. In some ways, he knew she considered him a father figure, as hers had never been much of one past giving her his name and genetics. Over time, John had given more of his time to work and less to Gwendolyn, which was one of the reasons he'd set her up with a young Dante Smith, the son of John's one-time closest friend. John had carried great influence in Dante's life, at least from his senior year of high school through his current age of 25. Trusting Dante to take care of his darling Gwendolyn hadn't been easy at first, despite the fact that Dante was the person John came the closest to trusting.

However, even with John's reservations about pulling back his involvement in Gwendolyn's life, he'd always made sure to keep tabs on everything, particularly Dante. When John answered the phone, hearing Gwendolyn's slightly panicked voice, his desire to protect her and fix her problems reemerged. As she spoke about her experience with Dante that evening, John felt a slight anger rise up in him, something he'd trained himself over the years to avoid. When she reached the end of the story, though, and explained that the crux of her worry came from the bloodstain and a strange phone call, which had apparently caused Dante to leave, John realized that it wasn't Dante that deserved his anger.

John remained silent for a few seconds, then calmly told Gwendolyn that he would take care of everything. She, of course, knew of Dante and John's friendship, so it wouldn't be a great leap for her to believe that John would simply talk to him. After hanging up the phone, though, John looked down at the sole picture on his desk. The picture was tattered and frayed, obviously aged poorly, despite being in a strong, classically wooden frame. John stared at the face in the picture, fighting the urge to speak to it, ask for guidance. John picked up the frame and turned it around in his hands a few times, allowing himself to process everything. When he went to place it back in its spot, he realized that the picture had been in place for so long that the color of the desk had faded, making it obvious were it belonged. There were many that questioned John's reasons for having a picture of Conner Smith on his desk. Despite their friendship, the few people that entered his office and knew John in any capacity would often ask why there were no pictures of Gwendolyn, Dante, some great lost love, but John knew what they really wanted to know was: "why is there a picture of Conner on your desk?" The answer, though, was never revealed, largely because it simply wouldn't be as interesting or scandalous as they'd have hoped. John simply missed his only true friend and often needed a reminder of why he was on his current path.

"Agent Dawson?"

John heard the voice of his young, overqualified secretary speaking through the intercom and finished the job of placing the picture back in its spot. He didn't have to push the button in order to know what she wanted, as he'd set the wheels in motion himself. Still, there were specific ways things had to be done, especially in a place like the Central Intelligence Agency. John sighed and readied himself, then pulled out several files that he needed for his next appointment. Taking one more glance at the picture on his desk, John pressed the intercom button with more force than typically required.

"Send him in, Janet, and hold my calls," John replied.

As the door opened, John stood up, straightening his dark blue tie, which somewhat clashed with his navy blue suit, though John had long since moved past the realm of caring what other people thought of his appearance. As senior special agent of the CIA, John was already on the fast track to advancement, though many would remark that at the age of 50, he was closer to the end of his career than the beginning. John leaned his 6'0" frame against his desk, allowing the illusion that his office was a relaxed environment. In truth, John simply didn't have the need or desire to play power games with his guest. As his superior and handler, John had all the power he needed, and since the visiting agent was bigger, stronger and faster than John, there was no sense in trying to make things appear otherwise.

"Dante, I believe we may have a slight problem," John said, not moving from his spot against the desk.

"Of course, sir," Dante said, standing at attention. "When I received the signal, I knew . . ."

"In my office, call me John," John said. "And I don't believe you did receive the signal, which is part of the problem."

"She called, didn't she," Dante said. "What did she say?"

"Have a seat, we have a lot to discuss," John said, moving away from the desk and returning to his office chair. "Yes, Gwendolyn called and informed me that you'd been acting strange tonight. She said she'd noticed several oddities, including a possible blood stain on your shirt, and you tearing out of the house after a wrong number on your cell."

"The stain . . ." Dante said, wincing. "Lyon got clipped in the Mills' case, and I guess I got a little blood on me patching it up. I didn't think Gwen noticed. What's she think? She doesn't think I'm having an affair, does she?"

"No, I believe she's more concerned you've gotten yourself into some type of trouble, though she couldn't quite come up with any feasible explanations for how an accountant could do so," John said, sliding the files across the desk. "I'll visit her later at home, handle things. Just be more careful. For now, you need to drop everything and get started on this immediately."

"John . . . I understand how vital it is to maintain our secrecy, but Gwen . . . you know we can trust her," Dante said. "Is there any way we can get approval to at least tell her I'm not an accountant? It's been five years, and I just . . . I hate lying to her."

"I understand, son. I truly do," John said, swiping his hand through his dark gray hair. "I have no doubt that Gwendolyn would do her best to keep your profession a secret, but it's too dangerous for her to know. Should she slip up and accidentally reveal that you're a CIA field agent to the wrong person . . . well, it's not just your life that would then be in jeopardy. Don't worry, I'll handle it."

"I get that, I . . ." Dante paused, staring at one of the pages in the file. "John, is this some kind of joke?"

"I see you've found the part that references aliens," John said, sighing. "I shared your skepticism . . . at least at first. We get hundreds of tips involving alien sightings and UFO landings a day, and obviously we treat them all exactly as you'd expect . . . as rubbish and tabloid nonsense. This, though . . . something's different about it. The mutilated bodies, the DNA left behind . . . there's something there. I need you to check it out, find out what's at the center, gather information, and, if necessary, deal with it with extreme force."

"Right, but . . . aliens?" Dante said.

"None of us believe that aliens are involved, but . . . someone is responsible for making it look that way," John said. "It could be a serial killer with a strange fetish, or it could be a matter of national security. Either way, Chicago's not a small place, and eventually this is going to get out and panic will ensue."

"Understood," Dante said, standing up. "Not that I'm complaining, but . . . doesn't this fall more in the FBI's jurisdiction?"

"Normally, yes, but these are special circumstances," John said. "That's all I can tell you. The rest is classified above your level of clearance. Familiarize yourself with the file. Your flight leaves in an hour. An agent will meet you at the airport and provide you with more information once you've arrived."

"I'm on it," Dante said. "John . . . about Gwen . . ."

"I'll handle this, too. Don't worry," John said. "And Dante, be careful. Like I said, something doesn't feel right about this one."

Once Dante had exited the room, John stood up and put on his suit jacket. The matter with Gwendolyn would need to be handled sooner rather than later, and John was fairly confident in his ability to throw her off the trail, while still maintaining Dante's cover. He had no intention of messing up their marriage, which meant that Dante's being out of town so soon after she'd had questions about his life would need to be handled delicately. John grabbed his briefcase by the door and then double checked his door lock before heading out into the main part of the office.

"Janet, could you please forward any important calls to my cell phone and send the rest to my voice mail," John said. "After you've set that up, take the day off tomorrow. I've got several matters that will require my attention out of the office, so I doubt I'll be here anyway."

"Thank you, sir, I'll get right on it," Janet said. "Oh, and you did receive a call during your briefing with Agent Smith. It was the strangest thing, he acted as if it were vital that he talk to you, but he wouldn't hold or leave his name . . ."

"I see," John said, feeling a tightness in his chest. "Did he say anything at all?"

"He muttered something about his phase or the phase . . . I'm sorry, sir, it was difficult to hear him. There was a lot of static on the line," Janet said.

"It's fine, Janet, I'm sure if it's important, he'll call back. Send that one through regardless," John said. "I'll see you the day after tomorrow."

John rushed away from his office, not waiting to hear anything else Janet may have had to say. As John had told Janet, he had several things to take care of, and waiting for his mystery caller to call back wasn't on the list for the night. John looked at the clock, seeing that it was almost 8:00 p.m. and wondered if Gwendolyn had eaten dinner yet. Of course, he could call and check, but he didn't want to add to her anxiety until he could finish thinking through Dante's cover story. John nodded at building security as he headed into the parking garage and made his way to his black Cadillac. Placing his briefcase carefully in the passenger seat, John sat silently for a moment, mulling over the day's events and wondering whether it was Dante or himself that were headed into the more perilous circumstances.

CHAPTER 4

DANTE

It had been over an hour since Dante had last spoken with John and was going on two hours since he'd last seen Gwen. No matter how hard he tried to focus on the mission files in front of him, he continually found himself looking out the window next to his first class seat on the plane, thinking about what Gwen must be thinking. From day one, Dante had argued the case for at least informing her that he was in the CIA. He trusted her completely, and it didn't hurt matters that she'd grown up around John, who no doubt had instilled in her the importance of keeping government secrets. Dante had no intention of revealing mission briefings to her or really doing anything past telling her when he would be going on a potentially dangerous mission. It wasn't that Dante had trouble understanding the need for secrecy, and John's case that knowing his true job would possibly put Gwen in jeopardy also made sense, but Dante just hated the feeling of lying to the woman he loved. Now that she knew something strange was going on, he felt the urgency to tell her becoming that much stronger. Of course, it didn't help matters that he'd had a headache since he'd left John's office, something he'd passed off as lack of sleep combined with stress.

"Excuse me, miss?" Dante said as the government assigned flight attendant answered his previous call. "Do you have anything for a headache? I don't need anything prescription strength, just . . . well, really anything will do."

"We carry Tylenol and Advil. Do you have a preference, Mr. Smith?" the woman replied, smiling brightly.

"Not really. Just bring me whatever's handiest," Dante said. "Maybe a glass of water, too. Thank you."

As the woman left, Dante rubbed his hands along the sides of his temples. For most of his life, Dante had managed to avoid any serious injuries or illnesses, but he'd always been susceptible to occasional massive headaches. They weren't quite migraines, but they were strong enough that Dante was willing to try almost anything to get rid of them as soon as possible. After just a few seconds, the flight attendant returned, happily handing Dante the pills and a cold glass of water, then heading back into the coach section. Once he'd taken the pills and finished the water, Dante closed the file folder, then forced his eyes to do the same. The flight would be over soon, and though he felt it unlikely that he'd be able to fall asleep, especially with a headache, the hope that sleep provided was worth the gamble.

The squawking of the plane's intercom system shook Dante out of his unexpected sleep. The sleep had been so deep that it took Dante a moment to figure out where he was. As he looked to his right, he could see the plane was making a steady descent towards an O'Hare runway, but there was still a nagging feeling clinging to him that he couldn't quite place. He felt as if he'd dreamed something important, something vivid, but the longer his consciousness forced him into a fully awake state, the faster everything slipped away. *The time is coming soon.* Dante jumped at the thought as it appeared in his mind, causing him again to look around the first class area just to make sure it was a thought and not someone speaking. The voice in his head wasn't his own, but it sounded strangely familiar. Dante struggled to remember anything from his dream, but the more he tried, the faster the details slipped away. *There's nothing you can do to stop it.* Dante closed his eyes again, rubbing them with his hands and straining to feel normal again. He took stock of the situation, calming himself with the notion that whatever voice he was hearing was simply a leftover effect from the dream. He resigned himself to never taking headache medicine again and then opened his eyes, just as the plane skidded along the runway, halting at the proper gate at the proper time.

"Sir, is everything okay?" the stewardess asked, showing concern in the way she tilted her head and scrunched her eyebrows.

"Yeah, I'm . . . yeah, just a strange dream," Dante said, shaking away the aftershocks. "Everything's fine, thank you."

The stewardess smiled and motioned for Dante to exit the plane, which he did along with the handful of other passengers in an orderly fashion. Dante briefly wondered whether everyone else on the plane was also from the CIA or another government agency, or if some were simply "normal" people unknowingly enlisted in aiding his cover. As the crowd dispersed and most headed towards the baggage claim, Dante clutched his briefcase and walked through the airport terminal, scanning everyone and everything for an indication of the agent he was supposed to meet. Even though it was only 10:00 p.m. in Chicago, Dante noted that the airport was nearly empty, which seemed somewhat odd to him, simply because he'd always imagined Chicago as a bustling, overcrowded metropolis.

Upon reaching the main area of the airport, Dante pulled out his cell phone to again check for any missed calls. Seeing that there weren't any, he called John. Part of him was glad for the excuse to check in on the situation with Gwen, though he was also concerned that things on his end weren't going according to plan. After a few rings, John picked up, and Dante stifled a small laugh as he realized John was already mid-sentence. Though John had an amazing military mind, there were occasionally signs of technological ignorance which Dante and most of the other agents found humorous, as long as they weren't in his presence at the time. They were always small, inconsequential things that never affected his job performance, but seemed to Dante as merely an indication that John was always more comfortable in the field than behind a desk.

". . . already on the scene. You should have gotten the message by now," John said.

"I'm sorry, the connection is a little spotty," Dante said. "Did you just say that I'm supposed to meet Agent . . . sorry, missed his name . . . at the scene?"

"Special Agent Lee. He's the lead agent on the case, and he seemed to feel it was necessary to coordinate with the Chicago PD and clear off a crime scene. There's been another murder," John said.

Dante closed his eyes and sighed, "Civilian?"

"Unfortunately," John said. "I've arranged for a taxi to take you straight to the Pier. It's shut down for the rest of the week, and we've managed to convince the Mayor to call it remodeling, but this is going to get out sooner rather than later. I need answers before it does."

"Understood. I'm on my way," Dante said, exiting the airport and heading straight towards the only taxi in the immediate vicinity. "Any more word from Gwen?"

"I'm on my way there now, son," John said, clearing his throat. "You're going to have to trust me on this one. I'll take care of it, but you need to keep your mind on the current situation. I'm afraid it's going to get worse before it gets better."

"I'm focused, just . . . tell Gwen I love her," Dante said.

"Of course," John said. "I'm pulling up to the house now. Don't worry, and, son . . . stay safe."

The connection was cut off from John's end before Dante had a chance to respond, which he'd come to expect. Though many of Dante's fellow agents saw John as cold, sometimes even callous, Dante knew that he simply showed his concern in less obvious ways. When John went so far as to tell someone to "stay safe," it was similar to someone else giving a caring, heartfelt message of support.

"Mr. Smith?" the taxi driver asked, opening the back door for Dante.

"Yes, sir. What's the ETA to the Pier?" Dante asked.

"This time of night, with traffic light . . . maybe forty minutes," the driver responded, getting into the driver's seat and wasting no time in heading out.

"Great," Dante said. "I hope you don't think I'm being rude, but I need to catch up on some reading for work on the way, so I'm gonna be pretty quiet."

The cab driver laughed, "Not been in many taxis, eh? No worries, Mr. Smith. I appreciate the notice, though. Basically two kinds of people that I take from the airport: rude and 'talk yer ear off.'"

Dante laughed politely and nodded his head, then waited for the driver to turn his attention back to the road before pulling out the case file and getting to work. He'd already familiarized himself with the most important details, but he still couldn't quite figure out where the "alien DNA" claims originated. The murders were gruesome, almost animal-like in nature, but it was nothing Dante hadn't seen too many times before on the news. Dante read each line of each page over and over again, trying to find some common sense explanation for everything. Of course, he knew he wouldn't find any real answers before he saw the crime scene, but he wanted to be able to keep pace with Special Agent Lee, who Dante knew was one of the Agency's best and brightest. He'd heard several stories about how Lee seemed to solve cases in the same amount of time it took most to read their briefings, and Lee's reputation for professionalism far preceded him. It was because of that reputation that Dante found it odd that Lee wouldn't have contacted him directly, but if the murder had happened during Dante's flight, it made sense that other things had been on his mind.

After several minutes, Dante put away the files and looked out the window, watching as the city raced past him. He'd been to Chicago once before, shortly after he and Gwen had been married. She had always loved the idea of big city life, and Dante had been willing to give it a shot. As a trial, they stayed for a week, and, aside from living in a hotel, they tried to do everything as they would have as actual residents. The experiment never reached its official conclusion, though, as Dante was called back to the Miami office on official business. He'd promised to keep the move on the table, and he fully expected her to revisit the potential decision again someday. Realizing that his mind was beginning to delve back into thoughts of John's explanation to Gwen, Dante refocused himself back on the case.. Watching the lights of the city and the L train occasionally flashing in and out of his view, Dante turned his thoughts to the part of the case that provided him with the greatest discomfort: the "alien" DNA.

Obviously, there was no way for a legitimate scientist to prove that DNA found on the scene had any alien qualities, aside from an inability to be categorized under known qualifications. Dante had no doubt that part of the reason he'd been called in, though, was the remote possibility that there was anything to the alien side of things. After his father died, Dante had heard all the rumors about Conner's supposed final mission with NASA. There were stories passed around like baseball cards about Conner being abducted, being probed and prodded, and even the occasional "theory" that he was still alive, but the government refused to look for him in order to cover everything up.

Once Dante had officially entered the CIA, he'd gotten so used to hearing the rumors, he expected to be taken aside and told which were true and which weren't. None of that happened, though. As an agent, Dante was treated, for the most part, as any other agent. No one seemed to care what had happened to his father, and, as time went on, Dante had even managed to drive away the insane ramblings about his father's alien involvement. Until today. Until this case. Despite what everyone on the outside believed, Dante had yet to meet anyone in any agency or branch of government service that had ever spoken of possible alien existence or any of the "Area 51" nonsense that found its way constantly into bad pop fiction. There had to be a reasonable explanation, and Dante fully intended on finding it.

Finally, the cab slowed to a halt in front of the public entrance to the Navy Pier. In his last trip to Chicago, Dante and Gwen had taken some time to visit it at night, mostly so she could ride the giant Ferris wheel, and that had served as their one and only tourist-like activity. It was strange to see it completely dark and devoid of life, though.

"I can take you to one of the parking garage entrances if you want," the cabbie said.

"Don't worry about it, I'd rather walk the rest of the way . . . get a feel for things," Dante said, opening the door and walking to the driver's side window. "What's the damage?"

"Already been covered. I guess whoever you work for has some kind of fancy prepay arrangement set up," the cabbie said.

Dante pulled out two crisp one hundred dollar bills and handed them to the cabbie, "Take this anyway. I'm betting some of those rude, rushed people you were talking about stiff you more often than not."

The cabbie looked at the cash, then waved it off, "My tip was included in the fee. Don't take me as all noble or nothin', I just . . . I don't want trouble from my bosses for it lookin' like I double charged."

"Between us, then," Dante said, forcing the money into the cabbie's hand.

"Thanks, I . . . thank you," the cabbie said. "You want me to hang around? Don't look like anyone else is around . . ."

"I've got it covered. I'm . . . I'll be staying around here. Close enough to walk. Have a good night," Dante scanned the inside of the cab quickly for the driver's license. "Phillip."

"Phil. Thanks . . ." the cabbie said. "Hey . . . be careful. No lights, this time of night . . . may not be safe."

Dante smiled, "If people keep warning me about my safety, I'm going to start to think there's a conspiracy against me."

Dante nodded his head and smiled, then waved as the cabbie left. Though it probably wasn't the strangest drop-off the cabbie had ever had, Dante wondered what he'd think of the situation when the news eventually broke about the murders in the area. Dante pulled out his phone and checked it, making sure he hadn't missed any messages from either John or Agent Lee, then followed the road around the side of the Pier towards the parking garage entrances. Immediately after rounding the corner, Dante saw a black SUV parked in the middle of the lane, the driver's side door and the hatch both open. The lights were on, though appeared to be dim, which meant the vehicle had been left on for a decent amount of time. Dante gently set his briefcase down inside the nearby tollbooth and drew his gun and pulled out a small LED flashlight. Holding the gun out in front of him with his right hand, steadying it on the flashlight held in his left, Dante slowly moved towards the SUV.

As he drew closer, Dante made sure to keep a few feet of space between him and the vehicle, in case someone was inside waiting for him. Seeing that it was empty, or at least appeared that way, Dante looked around then took a few steps closer. With each step, Dante paused and listened, paying special attention to his peripheral vision in case there was any movement around him. Once he made his way to the open driver's side door, Dante peered in the back seat, shining the flashlight in and making sure there were no surprises. A slight buzzing sound seemed to be coming from the front seat, and Dante took a step back and quickly moved to his left, looking all around him, then shining the flashlight towards the area of the apparent noise. Laying there in the front seat was a cell phone, set to vibrate. Dante stepped forward and picked it up just as it stopped buzzing. Setting down the flashlight for a second, Dante slid the phone open, thankful that it wasn't locked, and saw that there were 5 missed calls. The most recent was from John, but before Dante had a chance to scroll through the rest, he heard a loud crash towards one of the parking garage entrances at the end of the access road.

Pulling out his own cell phone with his left hand, Dante began scrolling through his contacts for the number to the local CIA offices. It would have been faster to use the verbal commands, but Dante felt the need to keep things as quiet as possible for the moment. *The end is inevitable.* The same voice from the plane tore through Dante's mind, bringing with it another major headache. Dante quickly blinked his eyes, trying to focus enough to place the call. The pain from the headache was so intense, that Dante didn't even feel the impact from behind that sent him barreling towards the ground face first. The only way he knew he'd been hit was that the quick tumble to the ground was followed with another sharp blow to the back of his head. As his consciousness began to fade, Dante attempted to roll over and catch a glimpse of whoever had attacked him, but it was too late. The last thing Dante heard before the darkness overtook him was the curious sound of deep, haunting laughter.

CHAPTER 5

GWEN

It had been hours since Gwen last spoke with Dante, and to say she'd worried herself into a frenzy would be putting it mildly. Gwen wasn't a worrier by nature, and in fact, it was rare that she wasted time thinking about negative scenarios. Her parents had been all but absent from her life through her early years, which was how she'd developed such a strong familial bond with her uncle John. Often, John's visits with her would include some unrequested advice about how to deal with her parents and her life. Though she'd never sought out the advice, Gwen always listened closely as John would explain to her that she was special and could easily grow to be anything she wanted, with or without anyone else's help. He would tell her that he would do his best to always impact her life, but that there would come a day when even he wasn't there. To say such a thing to a young child would seem inappropriate to some, but Gwen understood that John was merely trying to help her grow into the best version of herself.

Now, as she sat alone at the kitchen table, all of the worry and dread that she'd managed to avoid over the years was spilling out through every inch of her body. Dante had never given her a reason not to trust him, so she still tried to cling to the hope that there would be a good explanation for his apparent disappearance. She'd tried calling the office, as well as his cell phone, only to find no answer from either. Once she'd given in and called John for help, he had promised her to check in on things, but even that promise from her beloved uncle seemed somewhat shaky at the moment. Gwen had no idea why she felt such obvious pangs of insecurity and worry at the moment. Dante was an accountant, not a police officer or firefighter. When he went to work, she took comfort in the fact that he was facing no danger greater than a paper cut or a misfired staple. Something about the stain on his shirt spoke volumes to her, though, and she simply couldn't get it out of her mind.

Realizing that she was making herself crazy for potentially nothing, Gwen stood up and walked across the cold linoleum floor of the kitchen, peaking out every window she came across. She stared out at the empty street trying to will either Dante or John to appear. When a cab slowed to a near stop in front of her house, Gwen felt her heartbeat begin to race, but she was soon relegated to disappointment again as the cab sped up and continued its journey. The sheer silliness of not knowing what to do with herself caused Gwen to reflect back to her wedding day, when she found herself continually staring at the clock, waiting less than patiently for her moment to walk down the aisle. It was Dante's mother, Becky, who had noticed Gwen's constant glances and stated simply and calmly, "a watched pot never boils." Gwen remembered staring at her for a moment, wondering whether she'd missed out on the rest of the conversation. Apparently sensing Gwen's confusion, Becky had gone on to explain that worrying and watching for something to happen would do nothing more than cause the time to seem longer. The water in the pot would boil when it was time to boil, no sooner, no later.

As they had at the time, remembering the wise words of Becky Smith somewhat comforted Gwen. She forced herself to reflect on her relationship with Dante, reiterating the trust and love they shared together. If there was any reason for her to worry, he would have told her. As for John, though he was out of the military now, Gwen knew that he kept himself busy, so it wasn't necessarily unexpected that he would lose track of time. Gwen sighed softly, then headed back to the kitchen and poured herself a fresh cup of coffee. She closed her eyes and drank the warm, highly caffeinated beverage and slowly began to return back to normal. She pushed the worry about Dante's possible bloodstain out of her mind and simply relaxed, waiting for the "pot to boil" on its own.

Like clockwork, as soon as Gwen stopped fretting over things, she heard a car pull up into her driveway. She continued sitting, listening to the engine idle for what seemed like several minutes before finally cutting off abruptly. Seconds later, John was standing at the front door, dressed in his Army dress uniform and standing at attention, as if Gwen were a fellow serviceman and not family. She opened the door, smiling slightly and led him to the kitchen, where he sat calmly and professionally, just as she'd come to always expect from him.

"Gwendolyn, I spoke with Dante earlier," John said, making eye contact. "In fact, I'm the reason he hasn't been returning your calls."

"What?" Gwen asked, louder than she'd intended, hoping she'd misheard.

"It's nothing you need to worry about, but when I contacted him, he was in the midst of some very pressing business. He wanted to drop everything and run home, reassure you that he was fine, but I convinced him that I could intercede, explain everything," John said.

"I don't . . . why would you do that, John?" Gwen said, finally taking a seat at the table across from John.

"Gwendolyn, there's something you don't know about Dante's job," John said. "Recently, he's begun doing some accounting work for the government. Helping to audit various branches, keep track of spending. It's all top secret, and he simply doesn't have the clearance to tell you about it. I promised him that I would explain it to you, but you must keep it to yourself, even around Dante."

"That's . . . well, I guess I understand. So the wrong number . . . that was . . . some sort of code?" Gwen said.

"Essentially, yes. That's really all I can tell you about . . ." John said.

"And the stain?" Gwen asked.

"Pardon?" John said. "I don't . . . what stain?"

"The bloodstain on his arm. I know I told you about it earlier. That's the main thing . . . I just . . . I can't figure out what it's from," Gwen said.

"Oh, yes . . . I recall now," John said, as his phone began to ring. "That's from an . . . excuse me, Gwendolyn, this is an important call."

Gwen nodded her approval to John, expecting him to simply answer the call and stay put. However, once he put the phone to his ear, he quickly moved through the kitchen and out the back door, not speaking until the door was shut firmly behind him. Gwen sat in place, not wanting to stick her nose in his business, but she could still see him as he paced back and forth in front of the window on the back door. She tried to read his facial expressions, but John had never been one to show emotion in any discernible way. The call could be anything from a death in the family to a wrong number, and John wouldn't have given any noticeable hint as to the subject matter. After a few more minutes of pacing, John rejoined her at the table, though Gwen felt as if something was different about him. He seemed to be avoiding eye contact, though it was tough to tell if he was doing it purposely or she was simply allowing her imagination to run wild.

"Everything okay?" Gwen asked, slightly raising one of her eyebrows.

"It was . . . a business call," John said. "I'm afraid one of my side interests has fallen on hard times, and I . . . well, I really must be going, Gwendolyn. I just wanted to come back in and assure you that everything is going to be just fine. Dante's an open book, and aside from the classified work, there's nothing he's keeping from you. I'm sure of it."

As John reached out and covered Gwen's hands with his own in a reassuring manner, she felt better. Even though he'd had his share of secrets over the years, Gwen knew that John always attempted to be there for her, just as he had been tonight. She smiled and sat there silently, closing her eyes and thinking to herself how silly she'd been to give in to such worries. When John began to stand up, patting her on the wrist, Gwen joined him and walked him towards the door, happy that she'd at least had a chance to talk through her worries with a trusted friend and family member.

"I can't thank you enough for stopping by, Uncle John," Gwen said, hugging him.

"It was really my pleasure, Gwendolyn. Perhaps next week, the three of us can get together for a nice dinner, perhaps a show," John said, turning to leave.

At the mention of dinner, Gwen was reminded of the way Dante had rushed out of the house earlier just before they'd gone to dinner together. Though she accepted John's explanation for that, she realized that he'd never gotten around to answering her question about the bloodstain. In fact, it seemed as if he'd purposely avoided it, and she'd momentarily forgotten about it with the distraction of his phone call.

"Wait . . ." Gwen said, taking a step out into the abnormally chilly night air. "You didn't tell me about the stain. Was it blood?"

Gwen watched as John halted his march towards the driveway, and she knew it wasn't her imagination that he had taken longer than normal to turn back around and face her. Though she had convinced herself not to give in to worry again, she suddenly felt an uneasiness that made such a promise extremely difficult.

"Blood?" John said, pausing, frozen in place. "I believe . . . yes, I believe he said that there was some sort of freak accident at his office. Nothing severe, just a tad messy. Dante, of course, was first in line to help the poor soul."

Gwen narrowed her eyes and maintained eye contact with John, going over his newest story in her head. Even with government contracts, there were very few things that anyone in an accounting office could do to cause themselves to bleed enough to require help. For the second time today, Gwen took note that someone was acting very strangely after a fairly short phone call, and she was beginning to wonder how much of it could actually be chalked up to coincidence. As she stood there, the silence hanging in a thick fog between her and John, Gwen began to theorize what kind of connection he may have with her husband, and why Dante would allow someone else to do his explaining for him.

"Where's Dante?" Gwen asked, crossing her arms.

"Gwendolyn, I told you, he's . . ." John said, his phone again cutting him off mid-sentence.

"You can take all the phone calls you want, but I want to know what you're not telling me," Gwen said.

"Gwendolyn . . ." John said, looking at his phone, his eyes noticeably growing wider. "I can't . . . you're imagining things. I'm sorry, I have to go."

"John, I know you better than anyone else, and I can tell when you're hiding something from me," Gwen said. "If you really have to go somewhere important, then you'd better answer quickly."

Gwen maintained her position, wondering if she was overplaying her bluff. For all she knew about John's current life, the phone call could be a matter of life and death, so she didn't want to stand in the way of something important or even personal, but she had to know why John was suddenly the middleman in her marriage. As the phone continued to ring, Gwen watched John intently, waiting for him to make the next move and either call her on it and walk away or finally give her the one thing he'd always been hesitant to give: real answers.

CHAPTER 6

JOHN

JOHN HATED THE FEELING OF being in a situation he couldn't completely control. It was rare that he was reminded of the feeling, but nearly every time seemed to involve either Gwendolyn or, much earlier in his life, her mother. Lowering his gaze from Gwendolyn's glare, John quickly glanced at his cell phone, confirming that someone from the CIA's Chicago office was seeking his attention. Though John knew that answering it in front of Gwendolyn would lead to an uncomfortable and unwanted conversation, he also knew that time was of the essence, and he couldn't afford to ignore it. Closing his eyes and silently cursing himself for not getting out of the house when he had the chance, John answered the phone.

"Status report," John said, hoping to end the call as quickly as possible.

"We've confirmed that Agent Smith arrived at the location, but there's still no word from either he or Agent Lee. Protocol states that . . ."

"You don't need to explain protocol to me, son," John said. "Hold off on sending a team in until I arrive. I'm heading out now."

"But, sir, either or both of the agents could be compromised. If we don't act swiftly . . ."

"I'm aware of the consequences, but this is a very delicate situation," John said. "Until recent events, we weren't even sure there was a case, so we absolutely need more information before we go in blind. Authorize a pair of assets to do a drive by, but by no means are they to stop, much less exit their vehicle. In the meantime, continue to attempt contact with both agents, and keep me apprised of any changes to the situation."

After a brief pause, the agent on the phone responded just as John knew he would, "Yes, sir. We'll be awaiting your arrival."

John hung up the phone, checking the time before placing it back in his pocket. To her credit, Gwendolyn hadn't moved from her spot, nor had she halted in her unwavering glare while she awaited information. Though it had been discussed on more than one occasion to allow

Dante clearance to at least inform Gwendolyn of his true job, John had always led the charge to keep her completely in the dark. It wasn't that he didn't think she could handle the information or respect the need from secrecy, but rather it was the opposite. John knew from experience that Gwendolyn was one of the most trustworthy and intelligent individuals he'd ever met, and there had been several times she'd proven each quality to him. However, John knew that once the cat was out of the bag, there would be no way to contain it again. Gwendolyn's life would be forever complicated and changed. Whereas now she would have to deal with the occasional inconsistency in one of Dante's stories, once she knew the truth, she would begin to spend sleepless nights, worrying and waiting for her husband's safe return, never knowing whether he was on a mission or not. Still, unfortunately for everyone involved, John's presence was needed elsewhere, and he had no more time for games.

"Gwendolyn, sit down," John said.

"Listen, this is my house, and I'm the one . . ." Gwen said.

"If you want to know more about your husband's activities, then you will do as I say for once in your life," John said, pausing to compose himself. "I understand where you are coming from, dear, more than you know, but unfortunately I don't have the time to do this any way but quickly and directly."

"Fine, but you'd better tell the truth this time," Gwen said, sitting down at the kitchen table.

"Before I'm finished, you'll regret asking me to do that," John said, taking the seat directly across from her. "I'll get straight to the point. Dante is a field agent for the CIA. I recruited him myself in college, though I'd had my eye on him for much longer than that. His job as an accountant is simply a necessary cover."

"Are you . . . what do you . . ." Gwen mumbled. "That call . . . is Dante . . . is he okay?"

"Dante is fine. I promise. He's on assignment out of town, though I'm afraid I can't tell you where. That call had nothing to do with him or his rather mundane assignment," John said. "Gwendolyn, I need you to understand the gravity of this situation. It is imperative that you continue aiding Dante with his charade. If the wrong people found out, then your life would be in jeopardy, as well."

"I . . . understand," Gwen said. "Can I . . . I need to ask one question, and I need to know you're being completely honest with me."

John checked his watch, then nodded his ascent, "You may ask, but regrettably there are some things you simply cannot know."

"I'm not going to pretend I'm even close to dealing with all of this, but . . . well, I need to know . . . you said you'd had your eye on Dante for a while," Gwen said. "Did you . . . were we introduced as part of some . . . some plan?"

"Of course not!" John replied. "Gwendolyn, I never wanted this life for you, but at the same time, I'd never met anyone with as much character as Dante. I can promise you that I weighed every possible scenario before deciding to introduce the two of you."

Gwendolyn looked into John's eyes, and he knew she was weighing everything he'd told her, trying to determine if anything had the echo of an untruth. The only thing John had lied about had been Dante's current assignment, which, if the call was to believed, could be much more dangerous than John had already anticipated. While he regretted lying to Gwendolyn yet again, he knew that nothing positive could be gained if she sat at home alone worrying about Dante's safety. If it turned out that her concern was necessary, then John would simply have to cross that bridge when he came to it.

"Go," Gwen said.

"Gwendolyn, I'm truly sorry . . ." John said.

"We'll have that conversation when you're not expected somewhere else," Gwen said. "I'll be fine . . . we'll be fine. Just go, handle whatever it is you have to handle. Please tell Dante to call me the second he can."

John stood, leaning over to hug Gwendolyn, "Of course, dear. Please, get some sleep. I'll be in touch, as will Dante."

With that, John left the room, walking quickly to his car and speeding off, for the first time in a long time actually wondering if he'd done the right thing. Shaking off any uncertainty that he was currently feeling, John placed a quick call to make sure a jet would be gassed and ready for his arrival and subsequent departure to Chicago. It wasn't a wholly unexpected trip, but it was one he'd wished to make under far different circumstances.

* * *

CHAPTER 7

DANTE

DANTE WOKE UP SEVERAL MINUTES before opening his eyes, choosing instead to listen to his surroundings, try to figure out if his captor was working alone or not. In the distance, he could hear someone whistling, but he couldn't make out any more than that. Slowly, Dante opened his eyes, squinting at his surroundings. Everything around him was pristine, metallic. There were six monitors positioned around a larger monitor slightly to his left. Turning his head slightly, Dante could see that, though the large screen was powered down, each of the smaller screens showcased a different news feed. To his right, behind another row of computers was a hallway, though it was impossible to discern what was beyond that. Dante strained against the ropes holding binding him to the uncomfortable metal chair, but they were too thick for him to even consider breaking free. His head pounding, Dante turned his head from side to side gently, hoping to relieve some of the soreness he felt.

Though his training had gone through the potential trauma of being captured and tortured by an enemy, Dante had never truly believed it was a danger. It wasn't that he didn't understand the importance and danger of his profession, but rather that he'd grown overly comfortable in the fact that things tended to always go his way. A brief thought of Gwen was quickly shaken from Dante's head, as he didn't want to be emotionally compromised at a time when he needed a clear head and a strong mind more than ever. Forcing himself to breathe normally and take stock of the situation, Dante prepared for the worst. From the hallway, Dante could hear the whistling grow closer with heavy footsteps added to it. He closed his eyes and forced his body to go completely limp, hoping to get a feel for his captor before things went to the next level, whatever that was.

"I know you're awake," the man said, his gruff voice carrying ahead of him the final steps into the room. "I know you much better than you know yourself, Dante."

Dante ignored the boasting from the man and continued to feign unconsciousness, though he was sorely tempted to open his eyes and catch a glimpse of the man that had gotten the drop on him. Fighting against every survival instinct, Dante remained unmoving, limply leaning forward in the chair and allowing the ropes to hold him in place. Dante could hear the man's footsteps come to a halt as he entered the room, a loud sigh coming just inches from Dante's current position. After a few seconds, the man walked past Dante and began messing with something behind him. Suddenly, all the noise and movement ceased, and Dante began to wonder if there was an exit nearby. Before he had a chance to pursue the thought, though, Dante felt a large hand grab onto his hair and yank his head back with such force that Dante couldn't stop himself from grunting in pain. With his ruse effectively ended, Dante opened his eyes, seeing for the first time the face of the man that he assumed had caught him by surprise at the Navy Pier.

The man's eyes were bright blue like Dante's, but they were devoid of any kindness or mercy. His face was pale, a large scar along his left cheek and several smaller ones along the right, though they disappeared into a neatly trimmed beard. The most terrifying thing about the man was the wide, toothy grin he flashed at Dante, though the smile clearly didn't match with the man's still-steady eyes. As the man let him go and walked around in front of him, Dante could see that he was slightly taller and more muscular than Dante himself, a fact made exceedingly clear by the tight black shirt the man wore, tucked into a pair of black dress pants. Nothing about the man's appearance startled Dante as much as the hypodermic needle he was holding in his left hand, though.

"That's better," the man said. "Now, let's skip through all tedious questions I'm sure you're planning to ask me. My name is . . . let's go with Ulysses for now. That seems to fit nicely, don't you think? I'm simply here to test you . . . to make sure you're ready for our arrival."

"What are you . . . what are you talking about?" Dante said, the pain from his never ceasing headache making it hard to focus.

"I actually have no issue with telling you everything right here and right now, Dante, but the truth is," Ulysses paused, filling the needle with a greenish hued liquid. "You're not going to remember any of this anyway, so I feel like we'd just be wasting time. Don't worry, though, you're going to live through this. In fact, you're going to come out of this better than you were before, assuming everything goes as planned."

"Where's Agent Lee?" Dante asked, his eyes never leaving the hypodermic needle.

"Fine, we'll play this game for a little while. Like I said, it won't matter in the long run," Ulysses said. "I'll do better than tell you where Agent Lee is . . . I'll show you."

Dante's assumption that Agent Lee was already dead was essentially confirmed by the way Ulysses answered the question. Still, the fact that Ulysses had gently placed the hypodermic needle back on the table was at least a momentary victory. As Ulysses left the room, Dante did another look around his immediate surroundings, hoping to find something he'd missed the first time. The fact that his head was pounding wasn't helping, though, and he knew there wasn't much time. With every ounce of focus and strength he could muster, Dante strained against the ropes that held his arms behind his back. Despite the fact that it was mostly a last ditch effort stemming from Dante's growing sense of panic, he actually felt like the ropes were starting to loosen. In the background, Dante could hear a door slam shut, followed by heavy footsteps which signaled Ulysses' impending arrival. Holding his breath, Dante strained again, pushing himself harder than he'd ever pushed. Much to his surprise, the ropes snapped, giving Dante use of his arms, which still left him at a disadvantage but was at least a positive step.

Taking a moment to rub the feeling back into his wrists, Dante savored his slight freedom, then realizing that Ulysses' footsteps had stopped, he quickly placed them behind his back again to wait for his opportunity. He waited patiently to hear Ulysses' steps once again, but there were no longer any sounds coming from the hallway. Dante craned his neck, trying to see a little further down, tilting his head, wondering what was happening. The pounding in his head slowed down to a dull and distant pain, allowing him to fully focus on straining to hear any movement from Ulysses. Without any warning, the body of Agent Lee came flying into Dante's view, slamming into the wall and crumpling into a broken heap. Dante screamed, more from the sudden reemergence of his migraine than from the horrible scene that had just unfolded in front of him.

"Would you like a closer look?" Ulysses asked, appearing next to the body and picking it up just enough to drag it towards Dante.

With a quickness that surprised Dante, Ulysses covered the distance from the hallway to the chair, laying the corpse of Agent Lee across

Dante's lap. Dante held in the impulse to shove the body away, hoping to hide his small victory from Ulysses a little while longer. Dante looked up at Ulysses, who smirked and took a step back, leaning against the table which held the needle. Dante looked down at the man who would have been his partner on the case, taking note of the horrible, bloody scars all over his face and neck. There were claw marks all over his clothes, and Dante could see matching scars peeking out through the holes in the fabric. There was no question in Dante's mind that Agent Lee had suffered his fate in the exact same way as the other victims from the file John had given him. The obvious assumption was that Ulysses had killed him, but the marks were animal-like in nature. Dante briefly wondered if the fluid in the needle would match the "alien DNA" found at the crime scenes, but in his current predicament, there was really no sense in drawing any more conclusions. Instead, Dante hoped to stall, maybe even through Ulysses off his game enough to get the upper hand somehow.

"Why? Why would you do this?" Dante asked.

Ulysses laughed, "Oh, how much easier your life would be if it had been me. No, I'm afraid things are much more complicated than that, Agent Smith. I believe you already know what happened to him. It was in the file."

"How would you know what's in the file?" Dante asked, legitimately concerned.

"I know everything about you. We're connected in a way that . . ." Ulysses paused, looking off into the distance. "There's not enough time to explain everything, so you'll have to take my word for it . . . for now. How's the headache?"

Dante remembered his dream from the plane, realizing for the first time that Ulysses' voice matched the voice he'd heard in his head previously. He was by no means ready to accept an alien explanation, but he'd seen enough in his job to know that there were things out there that couldn't be explained easily. However, in Dante's experience, he knew that somehow, someway everything could eventually be explained logically.

"I suppose you want me to believe that you've been in my head," Dante said.

"I don't actually care what you believe," Ulysses said, standing up and making his way back to Dante.

Dante held himself in check as Ulysses moved closer. As he reached down to grab Agent Lee's body, Dante grabbed Ulysses left arm with his own left hand, then with his right punched Ulysses in the throat. Quickly sliding Agent Lee's body off while maintaining his grip on Ulysses' arm, Dante reached behind Ulysses' head and slammed it down onto Dante's knee. The quick and surprising turn of events clearly staggered Ulysses, as he fell backwards clutching his face. Dante wasted no time in going to work on the ropes binding his legs, hoping that if he could get himself free and out of the chair he'd be able to subdue Ulysses fully. Before he had a chance to move on with his plan, though, Dante's headache worsened even more. The inside of his skull felt as if it were on fire, unrecognizable images flashing through his mind at incredible speeds. The pain was so intense that he didn't even notice Ulysses now had one hand holding Dante's throat.

"Enough of the games," Ulysses said, as he plunged the needle past his hand and into Dante's neck.

As the fluid drained into Dante's bloodstream, everything seemed to slow down around him. The cloud of pain momentarily lifted, then once again worsened as everything slowly went to black around him. Dante swung wildly, hoping to at least do some damage before he lost consciousness, or perhaps his life, but Ulysses was nowhere to be seen. In the distance, Dante could hear a low, guttural growling, but before he could force himself to turn towards it, everything faded.

INTERLUDE

CONNER SMITH PACED NERVOUSLY AROUND the empty waiting room, proving to be every bit the stereotypical male in his current situation. Though his wife wasn't pregnant, they each had high hopes that was the reason behind their most recent appointment, this time at the doctor's request. Conner idly checked his watch, knowing in the back of his mind that he needed to get back to the base and continue preparing for his upcoming mission but not caring about anything other than the health of his wife at the moment. Conner sighed heavily and finally took a seat, picking up and leafing through every magazine in his immediate vicinity, though his focus remained on listening for even the slightest sound that may indicate his wife's appointment was finished. Nearing 40, Conner had his doubts about having and raising a child, but Becky had wanted it so badly for so long that her desire had finally rubbed off on him. They both knew that time wasn't on their side, which is what gave such great importance to their most recent trip to the doctor.

Tossing the magazines aside, Conner stood and walked over to a mirror mounted on the wall and stared at the most recent gray hairs peppering his otherwise jet black hair and beard. He'd spent a lifetime serving his country in the Air Force, then eventually moving on to NASA once his years of schooling began to match his age. John, ever the loyal friend, had urged him to take a desk job, one with more power and influence, but Conner loved the feeling of flying too much to give it up, although having a child would probably change that mindset. The small click of the door handle turning tore Conner from his thoughts, as he moved quickly towards the noise just as the doctor made her way into the room. Becky appeared just behind the doctor, her demeanor telling him everything he needed to know about how the appointment had gone.

"Becky . . ." Conner said, reaching out instinctively for her hand.

"Could you tell him, Doctor? I . . . I just can't . . . not right now," Becky said, leaning her head forward onto Conner's chest and crying silently.

"Of course, Mrs. Smith," Doctor Simmons said. "Mr. Smith, it seems that there is an obstruction . . ."

"Just cut to the chase, Doctor. What do we need to do to fix whatever it is that's keeping us from having a baby?" Conner asked, holding his wife tightly.

"Mr. Smith . . ." Doctor Simmons paused, looking at Becky then back to Conner. "I'm afraid it's not a strong possibility. As I told your wife, though, there are other options, such as adoption that . . ."

"Thank you, Doctor. I'm sure you've done your best, but I'll be seeking a second opinion on this. A third . . . a fourth . . . we're not giving up," Conner said, leading Becky towards the door.

Conner allowed the door to slam behind him, never stopping to listen to any response from the doctor. He had no problems with adoption, if that were the only possibility, but he was not accustomed to accepting defeat on anything, much less something so important to both he and his wife. As he helped Becky into the car, he wiped the tears from her cheek and, sweeping her long, wavy brown hair out of her face, kissed her on the forehead. As cliché as it sounded, Conner truly believed that she had only grown more beautiful with each passing day of their marriage. Her skin had paled and showed a few signs of aging, but her hazel eyes still made his heart skip a beat every time they locked on his own. He closed the door gently and walked around to the driver's side, pausing for a moment to gather himself before sitting next to his bride. He knew that now, more than ever, she needed him to put on a brave face, attempting to give her an optimistic outlook on their current circumstances. He breathed a heavy sigh and sat down, immediately reaching out for her hand.

"What time were you supposed to meet with John?" Becky asked.

"Don't worry about it," Conner said. "John owes me a favor or two, so I'm sure he'll cover for me. I'll just call him when I get home and . . ."

"Go. Drop me off at home. I'm going to make some calls, look into the idea of adopting," Becky said. "I know what you're thinking, but this isn't one of your missions. It's my body, Conner. I'm just too old, too tired. I think it's time we let this dream go, move on to the next one."

"Becky, I promise you, I will find a doctor that can help us. I have connections that . . ." Conner said.

"Don't," Becky said. "We've both known for a while that this just isn't in the cards for us. Lots of people adopt, and I'm sure it will be . . . it will be no different than having our own . . . baby. Maybe God's just making his will for us more obvious now."

Conner closed his eyes for a moment as he started the car. He knew his wife well enough to know that there would be no point in arguing with her this soon after the disappointing news from the doctor. As she'd said, adopting wouldn't be so bad, and he knew in time they wouldn't even think of an adopted child as any different from a biological one. Still, she was right that it wasn't just another mission, something he could tear through with sheer force of will. He would need to take some time, figure things out on his own before putting her through another doctor's appointment with more potential disappointment.

Conner started the car, then silently lifted her hand to his mouth and kissed it before letting it go to shift gears and head home. He would do as she said and drop her off, though once he arrived at the base he'd make a quick call to the neighbors to make sure she wouldn't have to be along for long. Despite what the doctor had said and how Becky had taken it, Conner began to feel more hope in the situation than he'd felt in quite some time. He couldn't wait to get to the base, talk to John and sort through his resources, find a way to fix everything for her, for them.

CHAPTER 8

DANTE

"DAD . . ." DANTE MUMBLED.

Slowly regaining consciousness, Dante tried to shake the cobwebs out, but the perpetual pounding in his head remained. Attempting to wipe his eyes, Dante realized that he couldn't move his arms. A sense of dread poured over him as he slowly began remembering his surroundings. The pain in his head was near crippling at this point, but he forced himself to focus, take stock of everything around him. He could neither see nor hear any signs of Ulysses, but the bonds holding him in place were much stronger this time, leaving him no choice but to remain in place and wait.

Looking over at the crumpled body of Agent Lee, Dante knew that there was more to this than met the eye, but he couldn't bring himself to believe in alien involvement. Ulysses was clearly a disturbed individual, and though Dante's involvement in the CIA was still fairly brief, he'd seen enough to know that there was a rational explanation for everything. More than that, he'd seen seemingly normal men capable of great evil and cruelty, and it was clear that, if nothing else, Ulysses was more than simply a normal man. As he sat there pondering the likelihood that he'd survive long enough to make an arrest, Dante's head began to clear slightly. There were images flashing throughout his mind, images of his parents from a long time ago, but trying to focus on them was similar to watching a movie with no sound and edited out of order.

"You'll gain more control with time," Ulysses said, walking back into the room. "Of course, it will be quite a while before you realize that."

"Why are you doing this?" Dante asked. "Why torture me instead of just killing me? The longer you keep me alive . . ."

"I have no intention of killing you, at least not yet," Ulysses said. "As for torture . . . well, let's just say your definition of torture should change quite a bit over the next few months."

"What is this 'great plan' you seem to have for me?" Dante asked. "I mean, if it's true that I'm not going to remember any of this, you may as well let me in on it."

"You seem to be clinging to the mistaken notion that I'm some boring human villain that gives away his advantage over the hero by arrogantly wasting his time explaining his 'evil plot,' Ulysses said, walking past Dante and out of his line of sight. "I'm afraid that simply isn't something that's in the cards for you."

"Let me guess," Dante said, straining against his bonds with everything he had left. "You're not really the villain here, just misunderstood . . . trying to change things for the better. Why . . . I bet all this torture is just to get me to see the bigger picture, maybe even join you?"

"No, I'm very much the villain, make no doubt about that," Ulysses said. "The problem with your little dream scenario is that I'm not human."

"Oh? So the 'alien DNA' must be yours then. Well, that explains everything. Thank you," Dante said.

"It's not quite as simple as that," Ulysses said, again appearing in front of Dante holding another hypodermic needle, this time filled with a black liquid. "I'll grant you that the murders that led you here were performed on my orders, but to be honest, I've yet to kill anyone."

"So what . . . you have aliens that do your bidding?" Dante said. "I'd sure love to see one of them before you inject me with . . . whatever that is."

"At the moment, they're only able to survive in this atmosphere for a few moments at a time, but don't worry, you'll get your chance," Ulysses said.

"You do understand how insane you sound, right?" Dante said. "'Sure, I've got a girlfriend, but she's on a modeling tour in France, so you can't meet her.' Look, let's be real, there's no way I'm ever going to let you get away with this, so either kill me or turn yourself in so I can get you some help."

"I have all the help I need," Ulysses said, slowly moving towards Dante.

Dante continued struggling against the bonds, hoping that somehow he would be able to break free before the needle again was inserted into his skin. However, the combination of being tied up for hours and the physical trauma he'd suffered prevented him from making any headway. Feeling the needle poke through, Dante held his breath, wondering if all of this had simply been an elaborate mind game before Ulysses finally killed him. As the substance inside the needle seeped into Dante's bloodstream, he could feel the pounding in his head resume. His body shook, and his vision became blurry, darkening around the outer edges, blotting out most of the lab. With the understanding that he was about to again lose consciousness, Dante attempted to focus on Ulysses, trying to keep some hold on the reality around him. As the darkness tore through his world, Dante could see Ulysses pick up a small object, which appeared to be a cell phone, though Dante was too far gone to fully make the connection. As the pain and the darkness mounted, Dante exhaled deeply and let himself go, allowing himself to again drift off into the nothingness.

INTERLUDE

When Dante's eyes opened, he was already running. He tried to stop, take stock of where he was, figure out why he felt so strange, but his body refused to cooperate. The heat of the bright lights flashing all around him was nearly blinding, but as Dante attempted to raise his hand to shield himself, nothing happened. Feeling a sense of panic begin to set in, Dante struggled to move his head, hoping to find anything with a reflective surface, but nothing would respond as it should. Dante was effectively a prisoner in his own body, and to make matters worse, he had no idea where he was or why it was happening.

Resigning himself to the fact that, at least for the moment, there was nothing he could do to fix his current situation, Dante chose to focus on every detail he could. The stench in the air was horrifying. It was like nothing he'd ever experienced before, and once he caught sight of the charred pile of bodies several feet in front of his current path, he realized why. Dante tried with all his might to stop or change course, but his body continued racing forward, diving directly into the pile of corpses, covering himself completely with the stench of burnt death. Every bit of his consciousness screamed out against the trauma, but his body remained perfectly still and quiet. Dante could see through a gap in the bodies, peering out the way he had just ran.

At first, all he could see was the continuous flash of the bright lights, which were now joined with the loud echoing sound of explosions in the distance. After a few seconds, Dante could hear another sound joining the distant din of the explosions. It was a low guttural growl, though it sounded less like an animal's and more like what a man would sound like after losing every shred of humanity in his voice. Just after another flash, Dante saw the lower half of the source of the growling, as two scaly, black legs appeared just outside the pile of bodies. Though his body remained still, Dante was able to see enough of the creature to tell that it wasn't human, as it crouched in front of him, its long arms giving way to five glistening black, knife-like fingers, all the same length. The creature growled again, and Dante wondered how long he had before it discovered him. He steeled himself for the confrontation, as much as he could with no control over his body, and allowed his thoughts to drift away to a silent prayer that Gwen had escaped whatever it was he was currently witnessing.

Everything shook, as another set of explosions went off, this time much closer. As Dante slowly began to recover from the ringing in his ears brought on by the nearly deafening sounds, he saw the creature rise and run back in the direction it had come. From the back, Dante could see that the creature looked almost human in shape and size, though the deep black made it difficult to make out any other distinct features aside from the claws and similar claw-like feet. Once the creature was out of sight, Dante could feel himself being lifted out of the piles, the stench assaulting his nose to the point that he felt dizzy. Before he had a chance to even begin to comprehend what had just happened, though, he was again racing off in the opposite direction of the creature. Dante wondered if he was somehow stuck in an incredibly realistic nightmare or if he'd just gone insane.

As the flashing lights began decreasing in intensity and number, Dante was able to gain a better grasp on his surroundings. Though he could still only see directly in front of him, he could see that everything was dark, the sky blocked out almost completely by what appeared to be ash and smoke. Immediately, Dante remembered reading about what would happen to the earth's atmosphere if enough nuclear weapons were discharged at once, which is what he now feared had happened. The last thing he could remember was sitting in a chair, bound by Ulysses. He struggled to think past that, but he had no recollection of either escaping or being rescued, and even if he did, he couldn't fathom how everything around him could have gone so badly so quickly.

Though there were few buildings in the area, nearly all of them were in various states of decay. There was no grass, or anything green, just what seemed to be miles and miles of broken pavement and dirt. As his body slowed down, Dante realized that he must have reached the destination he'd apparently been seeking. Turning through an alley, marked on each side by gutted out brown and black buildings, Dante was now walking slowly, still focused directly in front of him. Finally, he stopped completely and turned right, a charred silver door now in his path. In his peripheral vision, he could see his hands move, touching the wall in front of him. With a soft whirring noise, the wall opened like an elevator door, and he stepped into the darkness, which completely engulfed him as the whirring noise returned and the door quietly shut behind him.

For a few seconds, there was nothing. No sound, no light, even the horrible smells from outside had disappeared. As Dante began wondering if something had happened to him, a bright, nearly blinding light filled his vision. As it lowered in intensity, Dante could see that he was standing in a long hallway, lined with shiny, silver walls as far as his eyes could see. Desperately, Dante struggled to force his body to turn, so he could catch a glimpse of himself, just to feel some sense of normalcy. His body again began traveling forward, though, heading down the long hallway, with no end to it in sight.

After a few feet, he stopped and briefly looked to his left, allowing Dante to get a brief look, though once he had, Dante wished he'd stayed in the dark. As he continued forward, Dante's mind was filled with nothing but the image he'd just momentarily witnessed. It was clearly his body, but it had aged several years, possibly decades. His hair was buzzed, still black but with streaks of gray visible around his temples. He'd grown a full beard, which was somewhat shocking, but it was the prevalence of the scars and wrinkles lining his face that had truly taken his breath away. For the first time in his life, Dante felt defeated, unsure of what had happened to him or why he couldn't remember anything that had led him to this point. He was so discouraged, that he barely noticed when he finally reached the end of the hallway and was standing completely still in front of what appeared to be a dead end, once again assaulting him with the reflection of a man he barely knew.

As he stood there, contemplating his sanity, a small bright green light shined directly in his eyes, though for some reason he didn't flinch. The light appeared to be bright enough to nearly blind him, but there was no discomfort at all. Once it disappeared, there was another whirring noise and the wall in front of him opened just as the outside wall had. Though it was dark, Dante could see shapes moving in the distance, which he soon realized were actual, living and breathing people. Just when he felt that he would finally get some answers, though, everything began going dark around him and the people in the distance became blurry, finally disappearing completely. Dante wanted to run, to scream, to do anything, but he remained motionless as the darkness overtook him and his consciousness slipped away.

✶ ✶ ✶

CHAPTER 9

DANTE

DANTE AWOKE TO A FAINT buzzing keeping time with a flashing green light. As soon as his eyes were opened, he flinched, looking all around in a panic. Realizing that he was still in the same room tied to the same chair, he slowly came to accept that he'd just had the most vivid dream of his life. On reflex, he lifted his hands to his face, attempting to wipe away the sleep and confusion. It wasn't until he was finished that he noticed his hands were no longer bound. Somewhat disconcerted by the flashing green light, Dante hesitantly attempted to stand. Though there were no more ropes keeping him from it, he'd been stuck in the same position for so long that it took greater than normal effort to keep from falling. He cringed as he put his full weight back on both legs, the tingling of his sleeping muscles amplified by his other various aches and pains.

Forcing himself to inhale and exhale slowly in an attempt to revitalize his body, Dante stood just in front of the chair, looking around his immediate vicinity, first for signs of Ulysses then for anything he could use as a weapon. The area had been effectively cleaned up, with the rope and the chair being the only signs of his encounter with Ulysses. Dante felt like he was standing on the set of a television show after cancellation. The bare bones of the room still existed, metal desks and chairs neatly in place, illuminated by the flashing green light. Taking his first steps since his capture, Dante eased forward, doing a once over around the room, while also trying to find the origin of the light and the buzzing.

Finding nothing of use, Dante quickened his pace and headed towards the hallway he'd seen Ulysses enter and exit throughout their time together. Out of habit, he reached for his gun, finding nothing but an empty holster. Every sense screamed at him to call for backup, but he could see no way of accomplishing that short of literally calling out, something that would give away his position. Of course, since he'd woken up free from his bonds, it was likely that Ulysses already knew he was free. Either he'd run off, leaving Dante alive for some reason, or he was still hanging back, allowing Dante the illusion of regaining some sense of control on his circumstances. No matter what, Dante had no intention of letting him get away with the murders, whether he'd been the perpetrator or simply the man in charge of the killer.

Once Dante was in the hallway, he could see three possible doors, two on the left side of the wall and one at the end, marked top secret. Dante quietly checked the first door, somewhat surprised that it was unlocked. He opened it just enough to be able to peer through the crack, listening for any sign of life. Just because Ulysses had been the only person he'd seen and talked to, there no reason to believe he was working completely alone. In fact, as Dante opened the door more and squeezed into the room, he remembered seeing Ulysses speaking on the phone with someone earlier. While there could be many possibilities for that phone call, Dante had learned through experience that the most likely answer was usually the correct one. In this case, Dante surmised that if Ulysses took the time to speak on the phone while in the middle of torturing someone then the call would have to be related to the situation.

Though the room was dark, the flashing green light provided Dante with enough visibility to see that it was also empty. It appeared to be some sort of kitchen, and, while it was also bare, there were still cabinets and a refrigerator in place. Dante checked everything, but the refrigerator and all the cabinets were empty. Heading back into the hallway, Dante tried the next door in line, finding it locked. He twisted the handle back and forth, pushing as much as he could without making a lot of noise, but it remained stuck in place. He felt as if he could force it open if he used enough strength, but he wasn't prepared to announce his presence so loudly, whether or not Ulysses had planned his escape.

Before trying to open the "top secret" door, Dante leaned in close, placing his ear against the door in a futile attempt to prepare himself for what might be on the other side. Finding that the door was too thick, Dante turned the knob, expecting it to be locked, as well. When it clicked and opened, Dante stepped through the door, into another dark room. He stood in place, allowing the flashing green light to provide him with a slight sense of where he was. The room was much larger than Dante had expected, stretching farther than he could see, though much of that was due to the way the walls merged with the darkness.

In the distance, Dante could see a faint light, so he began slowly and carefully heading towards it. As he did, he realized that he was surrounded by large cylinder-shaped metallic objects, but the flashing green light wasn't strong enough to allow him to see more than the shape. There appeared to be hundreds of the cylinders, but as Dante made his way closer to try to figure out what they were, he heard a loud growling from the darkness behind him. Immediately, he was reminded of the creature from his dream, as he'd hid amongst the bodies. Slowly turning around, Dante found that his fears had come to life, as he was standing face to face with the scaly, black creature, looking just as it did in his dream.

Not taking the time to work out how this could be possible, Dante jumped on the offensive, punching the creature in the face. The brash move seemed to surprise the creature more than injure it, as it fell back slightly, barely keeping its balance. With no desire to find out how tough the thing was, Dante turned and raced back to the door. Before he made it, though, he felt the creature's grip squeezing his left arm, effortlessly flinging him into the same door he'd hoped would provide an escape. The impact drove the breath from his body, and he stumbled in his attempt to regain his footing. The silence of the creature's movements, save for the occasional growl, was more surprising and disorienting than the strength and viciousness of its attack. Dante managed to slide out of the way of what could have been a fatal claw swipe from the creature, but its backhand caught him, driving him back into the door once again.

Kicking out blindly, Dante managed to connect with the creature's abdomen, knocking it away with as much force as he could muster. He scrambled to his feet and ripped open the door, shutting it behind him just as the creature leaped. Dante knew that the door would only provide him with a moment's respite, though, so he raced back to the lock door and lowered his shoulder, slamming into it repeatedly until it gave away. He shut the door behind him, backing away and preparing himself for the creature's entrance. As he backed up, his foot brushed something, knocking it back and causing a muffled clanging noise. Dante looked down towards the noise, the flashing green light allowing him to see what appeared to be a long, metal blade.

Since there was no handle, Dante cautiously picked it up, as he couldn't tell if it was sharp or dull from the small amount of light available to him. It was almost like a chisel, as it had an edge, but wasn't sharp enough to cut through anything. Dante picked it up and braced himself, hearing the low, guttural growling of the creature just outside the door. Just when he thought the creature had chosen to pass the door, it came flying off its hinges towards Dante, who barely moved out of the way. The creature leaped into the room, wasting no time in renewing its attack. Dante swung the metal object like a bat at the creature's head, knocking off its leap and sending it crashing into the wall next to him.

Dante considered running again, but he was beginning to feel as if there was nowhere for him to go. As the creature shook its head and turned around, Dante prepared himself for an all or nothing attempt at ending the fight. Dante braced himself as the creature again leaped towards him, though instead of moving or swinging, he stabbed the metal object forward, the force of his strike magnified by the creature's momentum. The creature screamed out as the metal object went through its chest, and Dante flipped it over him, letting go of the metal object and allowing both it and the creature to fly out into the hallway, crashing into the ground with a sickening thud.

Racing out to press his advantage, Dante grabbed the metal object and ripped it from the creature from its back. The creature screamed again, as a black liquid poured out from each side of the hole that now existed in the center of its body. As Dante attempted to finish things by stabbing through the creature's head, it rolled over and reached out, grabbing his right arm and squeezing so hard Dante lost his grip. Dante silently prayed as the creature stood to its feet and glared at him with its pupilless black eyes, its lizard-like tongue licking along its long, sharp teeth. Dante tried to swing at the creature with a left jab, but it caught his left arm, as well, squeezing both and forcing Dante down to his knees in agony.

Rapidly losing hope, Dante held his gaze on the creature, trying to force his arms free, to no effect. In the distance, the buzzing stopped, as did the flashing green light, giving way to bright fluorescent lights. Dante heard footsteps behind the creature, though it seemed to be too intent on its impending kill to notice. Though all he saw was a blur, Dante heard a slight whoosh sound as something sliced through the creature's neck from behind, its head toppling off to the side. With the grip loosened, Dante ripped his arms free and scattered back, wondering what threat was upon him now. Instead of an attack, though, he heard the unexpected sound of clapping, then laughter as Ulysses kicked the creature away and extended his hand.

"For a moment there, I honestly thought you had him," Ulysses said.

Dante ignored the outreached hand and stood up, "What . . . what was that?"

"I believe you referred to it as an alien earlier, though I'm guessing you believe in it quite a bit more now," Ulysses said.

"That stuff you injected me with . . . it's . . . it's messed me up, hasn't it?" Dante asked. "I'm hallucinating."

"All that did was give you a glimpse of the future, magnify abilities you already possessed," Ulysses said. "Anyway, it doesn't matter if you believe in aliens or not, because our time here is done."

Dante opened his mouth to speak, but nothing came out. He felt a wave of drowsiness sweep over him, as Ulysses began moving towards him. He tried to stay standing, fight for his life, but, just like his dream, nothing was working the way it should. Dante fell to the ground, still trying to speak, to move, to do anything, but all he could do was watch as he was dragged back towards the "top secret" room. As he lost consciousness, he looked up again at the face of the man dragging him, but he realized that he could no longer recall his name. It was with that question that Dante's mind once again gave way to the darkness.

CHAPTER 10

JOHN

As John and his team pulled up to the abandoned SUV at the Navy Pier, he tried to prepare himself for the worst. It had been nearly a full day since Agent Lee had checked in, and no one had heard from Dante in several hours. John exited the passenger seat of the black Cadillac and drew his weapon, standing back while the other three agents surrounded and investigated the SUV. John wasn't as familiar with the Chicago branch as he should have been, though he'd heard several positive reviews about Special Agent Scott Henderson's field prowess. He'd been the only member of the team John had personally selected, hoping that Henderson would live up to the hype if things got hot.

"We've got a body," Henderson said, motioning for John to join him.

John raced to his side and knelt down next to the corpse, holding his breath as he gently rolled it onto its back. Eyes wide open, the corpse of Agent Lee stared back at John. He shook his head and stood up, allowing the other two agents to cover up the body with a tarp.

"Rigor mortis has already set in," John said. "He was dead when Dante arrived."

As John finished speaking, he heard a slight thud from inside the parking structure. All four men checked their guns, then headed towards the noise. Agent Henderson stood next to the wide open garage door, peering inside as one of the other agents raced to the other side of the door. John motioned for the third agent to stay with the body, then moved through the door, gun drawn, fully trusting the other two men to have his back. This section of the garage was completely empty, save for another body leaning against the back wall, next to the emergency exit door. John immediately recognized that it was Dante, but he maintained his composure, keeping his gun steady and checking each side as he slowly walked towards him.

As John knelt down and checked Dante's pulse, he could hear the other two men doing a sweep of the immediate area. John hadn't realized that he'd been holding his breath again, releasing it in the form of a loud sigh as he found Dante's pulse, which was slow but steady.

"All clear. Go call it in, then you and Smith run a quick sweep in the area," Henderson said to the other agent before joining John. "This your man?"

"Yeah, he's been put through the wringer, but he's steady. Something big went down here," John said. "Help me get him to the car."

Making sure not to jar Dante any more than necessary, John and Henderson carefully lifted him to his feet, putting his arms around their shoulders and walking slowly towards the car. Once they reached the car, John struggled to hold him upright as Henderson opened the door. Dante's muscle mass made him much heavier than John, especially when being unconscious made him dead weight. As the two men lowered Dante onto the backseat, John heard the other agents return, though he knew before they said anything that they'd found nothing. John stayed with Dante, while Henderson took the other two agents back to Agent Lee's body. All four of them were well aware of what would happen if they weren't able to clean up the area before the sun came up, whether it was blocked off or not.

"John . . ." Dante said weakly, his eyes still closed.

"You're going to be fine, son," John said, kneeling down and leaning against the open car door.

"Why are you . . ." Dante coughed. "Why are you here?"

"You went off the grid, so I came to find you," John said. "Get some rest, I'll debrief you after we get you treated."

"Nothing . . . to tell," Dante said, barely above a whisper. "Just got here . . . found Lee's body . . . hit from behind. Didn't see him. How'd you get . . . here . . . so fast . . ."

"Dante, it's almost morning, you've been gone for hours," John said.

"Just got here . . ." Dante said.

John stayed still for a moment, waiting to see if Dante had anything else to say, but it soon became clear he was out again. Although he would have several more questions once Dante was stable and awake, John felt fairly certain that Dante had just told him all he knew.

* * *

CHAPTER 11

DANTE

It had been a full day since Dante had been found at the scene of Agent Lee's murder. At first, everyone had kept their distance, giving him time to recuperate, but once word spread that the doctors had listed his injuries as non-severe, all that changed. John had been the first visitor, giving Dante his one and only pleasant surprise of his recovery time. Despite always warning Dante against it, John had told Gwen about his true occupation. Of course, he'd had to leave some things out, and she had no idea his current mission had been dangerous, so when he called her, he had to make her believe he was simply deep under a pile of paperwork. Regardless of the lie, Dante felt a huge weight lifted off his shoulders.

After his all too short conversation with his wife, Dante had been left alone again to recuperate, though his rest was broken up several times by various doctors and nurses entering and exiting his room. Dante had no idea if he was in an actual hospital or somewhere in the Chicago branch, and he didn't care. He wanted to get through the medical checks, then go through the debriefing and finally get home to Miami. He'd begun giving serious thought to his career and where it was going, but his mind kept replaying the events of the previous few days. Something about the timeline seemed off, and he had a nagging feeling that there was something he was missing. Finally, after another parade of doctors had entered and exited his room, John walked in and stood at the edge of his bed, the same serious look on his face that always resided there.

"Feel up to talking about what happened?" John asked, though Dante knew that his answer wouldn't affect the conversation one bit.

"Let's get it over with so I can get home," Dante said.

"Understandable," John said. "Walk me through what happened."

"After the plane landed, I took a cab to the Pier. I couldn't have been there more than five minutes when I found Lee's SUV, then his body. I checked it out, let my guard down . . . stupid rookie mistake . . . and boom.

Next thing I know, I'm in the backseat of your car, and everyone's acting like I've been gone for years," Dante said.

"Not years, but we have the plane landing at 17:32, and we didn't find you until 4:15," John said. "Being generous with the cab ride, that's still roughly six hours of you being unconscious."

"I don't know what to tell you, John. That's exactly what happened. I guess whoever it was just hit me in the right place," Dante said.

"The length of time you were unconscious isn't really the question, son," John said. "We can assume that whoever hit you was the same person that killed Agent Lee, and more than likely the same person responsible for the other murders. So why let you live?"

"I don't . . . I don't know," Dante said, rubbing his temples and trying to ease the sudden headache. "Maybe he was in a hurry, or maybe someone else was in the area . . . I don't know. I wish I did."

"Is there anything you're leaving out? Any minor detail, something about your trip that seemed off?" John asked.

Dante thought back, again retracing his steps from the plane to the Pier. Overall, it had been a fairly mundane trip, at least until he found Agent Lee's body. There had been no warning before the attack, but John was right in questioning why Dante was still alive. It was dark, the Pier was completely blocked off, even with traffic, the road was far enough away and the view obscured enough that the attacker would have been able to kill him quickly and with no hassle. None of it made sense, and Dante wondered if it ever would.

"I had a weird dream on the flight, woke up with a headache, but nothing after I landed," Dante said. "John, I get that this doesn't add up . . . what's the word out there?"

"You're not a suspect in Lee's murder if that's what you're asking," John said. "Autopsy confirmed that he'd been dead long before you arrived, although there were some strange bruises that seem to have appeared post mortem. Regardless, we just want to catch this guy, and you're the only lead we've got. Crime scene was completely clean."

"Maybe it really is aliens," Dante laughed, then immediately regretted it as an image of Lee's corpse flashed in his mind.

John cleared his throat, "I'm going to push for your immediate release and book your return flight. I'm going to stay behind, do a little more digging."

It wasn't lost on Dante that John had stiffened up even more than usual at the mention of aliens, even though it had been a joke. Dante wondered what information John was keeping from him, but more than that, he wanted to get home. In fact, Dante realized that it was more than that. He wanted to stay home.

"John . . . I think I'm done," Dante said quietly.

"Of course, son, you've done more than enough here, and . . ." John said.

"No, that's not what I mean," Dante paused, wondering if he was about to make a big mistake or finally make the right choice. "You're right. There's no reason for me to be alive right now. Whoever the attacker was, he had me dead to rights, and it's a miracle that I'm . . . I could have left Gwen alone. I can't do this anymore."

"Dante, son . . . you've just had a traumatic experience, you're not thinking clearly," John said, sitting down on the edge of Dante's bed. "Take a week off, go somewhere with Gwendolyn. It's completely understandable that you need some time away, but don't make a rash decision that you're going to regret in a month."

"Did you know that we're trying to have a baby?" Dante asked. "I can't . . . I grew up without a father. I'm sorry, John, but this isn't a rash decision. I hope you don't think I'm a coward, but . . . well, I don't really care either. I loved my father, what I remember of him, but I don't want to end up like him."

Dante flinched slightly as John lowered his head silently. Though John kept most of his life a mystery, Dante knew that he'd been close friends with his dad, and his death obviously still ate at John each time Conner was mentioned. Dante waited silently, preparing various rebuttals in his head for whatever arguments John raised.

"Being injured in the line of duty combined with your immaculate service record, regardless of how long it is," John paused, meeting Dante's curious stare. "I'll make sure the Agency takes care of you."

"Wow. I expected more of a fight . . ." Dante said, only half-jokingly.

"Conner Smith was a great man, and he gave his life to this country. We should all be proud of him, of his sacrifice," John said. "But I'll never forget the look in Becky's . . . in your mom's eyes when I delivered the news of his death. I hate to lose you, son. You're near irreplaceable, but . . . well, I love Gwendolyn too much to ever . . ."

For the first time in his life, Dante witnessed John so overcome with emotion that he couldn't even finish his sentence. He reached out and placed a hand on John's shoulder, nodding his head that he understood what he'd been about to say. Once the moment had passed, John stood and saluted Dante, then turned and left the room as if nothing had happened. Despite the fact that he'd loved working in the CIA, Dante felt no sense of loss as he thought about what his life would look like now. Pulling the IV tubes from his hand, Dante stood up and dressed. He looked in the mirror, and despite the faint bruises and scars on his face and the fact that he had no idea what he'd do with his soon-to-be spare time, Dante felt that his life was finally going to be everything he'd always hoped.

* * *

CHAPTER 12

GWEN

It had been nearly two weeks since Dante had come home promising Gwen that he'd quit the CIA. Even though she'd only known about his true employment for a day at that point, she had felt an overwhelming since of relief with his announcement. For the first few days, whenever he left the house, she'd spent time worrying that he was merely brandishing a new cover story, but each time he came home smiling shortly thereafter, the worries were pushed from her head. They'd spent a little time talking about his time with the Agency, but he'd not gone into detail, which she knew was more for her sake than that of national security.

At the end of the first week, everything changed. Dante complained of headaches so severe that he often couldn't move without grimacing, but no matter how many times Gwen suggested it, he refused to go to the doctor. Gwen began taking notes of the frequency and magnitude of his headaches, with the plan that she would talk to a doctor herself if they continued much longer. She would never forget the first time he collapsed, screaming, only to wake up a few minutes later unaware that anything had happened. She'd begun reading about possibilities like post-traumatic stress disorder, hoping to find something that fit and would be treatable.

It had been a few days since Dante's last reported headache, but as Gwen sat, staring at her pad of paper with notes about his condition, she couldn't shake the feeling that it was merely the calm before the storm. She'd called John earlier in the morning, while Dante was still asleep, but he'd echoed much of the same sentiment that Dante had over the previous two weeks. There were times that Gwen didn't fully trust John, especially after finding out that he'd been lying to her for years about his and her husband's professional connection. However, this wasn't one of those times, as John seemed genuinely concerned but still fairly positive that Dante would be fine. He'd promised her that it was a common occurrence for someone leaving such a stressful, demanding job, and since she hadn't seen any additional health defects, she chose to believe him.

After hanging up the phone, Gwen busied herself around the house. Summer break and just started, and while she would still have meetings and planning sessions to deal with, her time was much less cluttered for a few weeks. Walking into the bedroom carrying a freshly finished load of laundry.

"No . . ." Dante said.

Gwen started, not expecting him to be awake, "You don't want clean clothes? Not that you'd notice. I remember that old jersey you used to wear every . . ."

"Please . . . don't . . . DON'T . . ." Dante said, quietly at first, then getting progressively louder until he ended with a nearly unintelligible scream.

"Dante?" Gwen said, dropping the clothes and racing to the bed.

When she got there, she knew immediately that whatever was happening wasn't a normal nightmare. His eyes were shut tightly, sweat pouring down from his face onto the pillow. She reached out, brushing his hair back gently, then resting her hand upon his forehead. Despite being clammy and dripping with sweat, his head was so hot that Gwen's hand instinctively recoiled. Gwen pulled out her cell phone, but instead of calling an ambulance, her mind seemed to be urging her to call John.

"John, it happened again . . . worse this time . . ." Gwen said into the phone, as another of Dante's screams punctuated her concern. "Meet us at the hospital . . ."

"Gwendolyn, I know you won't understand this, but don't call anyone else just yet. I'm nearby. I'll be there in a few minutes," John said.

"John . . . you're not seeing him, he's . . . I have to . . ." Gwen said, sounding calmer than she felt.

"I know what's wrong, and I can fix it," John said. "Trust me. Please, Gwendolyn. It's what's best for Dante."

"You've got five minutes, then I'm calling 911," Gwen said.

After hanging up the phone, Gwen quietly walked into the adjoining bathroom and stared at her reflection in the mirror for a moment, contemplating whether she should ignore John's warnings and contact the hospital anyway. As she turned on the faucet and ran a cool, wet washcloth across her face in an attempt to wipe off the worry, she heard Dante's cough, followed by a creaking warning that he was attempting to get out of bed. She raced back and watched silently as Dante slowly picked himself up out of bed, nodded in her direction and crept past her to the bathroom, shutting the door behind him. She tried to remember what their lives were like before he started having these problems, but it was getting increasingly difficult, even though it had only been a matter of weeks.

When Dante came out of the bathroom and walked towards her, the first thing she noticed was that the glimmer was gone from his light blue eyes. The smile and laugh that had played a part in her attraction to him was now replaced with a worried, and sometimes pained, expression. Before he could speak, she reached up, standing on her tiptoes, and kissed him softly on the lips.

"Gwen, I know you're worried. Honestly, I am, too. I just . . . I don't know what's happening to me. The visions are tearing me apart inside. They're always intense, but this time . . . this time was different," Dante said. "This time I heard a voice. Maybe I'm . . . what if I'm going crazy?"

Dante pulled away from Gwen and turned around, visibly shaken. He ran his hand through his black hair, and then along his goatee, which was something he always did while thinking, though she had a hunch it was involuntary. Her mind was racing, as she tried to think of the perfect words to say to ease his mind, to let him know he wasn't going crazy. The problem, though, was that the more she knew about his headaches and visions, the more she worried that it might be a possibility. He'd told her of intense dreams he'd been having, but she knew he was holding back, trying to protect her like he always did.

"Can you talk about it?" Gwen said, rubbing his back, trying to alleviate the tension.

"I think . . . I can try," Dante said, tilting her face towards his and running his fingers through her silky blonde hair. "We should probably sit down, though."

* * *

CHAPTER 13

DANTE

DANTE WATCHED AS A MIXTURE of love, worry, and even fear passed over Gwen's face as he spoke. In the five years they'd been married, he'd never once questioned her desire to stay with him through sickness and health and insane, head-pounding visions and dreams, but he often questioned why she still desired it. By anyone's standards, she was a beautiful woman, young, blonde, and she kept in shape. He loved that she wasn't obsessed with her looks or always looking to the next diet fad to reach some obscene level of skinniness. She had always been supportive through dating and school, through career changes, and even through all of this, but part of him wished for her sake that she would grow to be fed up and leave him to his misery and find the happiness he was currently unable to give her. Still, that wasn't the woman he married, and he was certain how this conversation would go.

"We can work through this together. Everything will be all right," Gwen said.

Gwen . . . I don't love you anymore. Leave. Maybe if he were stronger, he could bring himself to speak those lies to her and save her. He had no idea why, but the more intense the dreams, the worse the headaches, the more Dante felt that something sinister was coming down the pike. Sitting next to Gwen on the bed, looking into her bloodshot eyes, he couldn't help but think back to his last mission. Though John and he had told her much of the truth, they'd never revealed how close Dante had come to death.

According to the timeline, he'd been unconscious for several hours, but he could tell from the way John had questioned him that there was a strong possibility something else happened during that time. His mind, however, was a blank. He remembered getting out of the cab, seeing Agent Lee's body, then nothing but darkness until he awoke in the back of a car with John's concerned gaze boring a hole into him. He could start out by telling Gwen all of that, possibly giving some context to whatever was going on with him now, but he was afraid it would further sever the only real family relationship she had with anyone besides him. He may not fully trust John, but he knew he'd always been there for Gwen, and for now, that was enough to give him the benefit of the doubt.

"Before you start . . ." Gwen paused, clearly uncomfortable with whatever she was about to say. "I called John. He's on his way . . . to check on you."

Dante closed his eyes and steeled himself against his first reaction, which was anger, not at Gwen but at John for no doubt pushing his way back into the situation.

"It's fine," Dante said, hugging his wife. "I think I'm okay now, but . . . well, it wouldn't hurt to hear his thoughts."

"He's going to hear my thoughts, too," Gwen said, her voice slightly muffled against Dante's chest.

"I'm sure he's terrified," Dante said, allowing himself to laugh for the first time in days. "Okay, so . . . are you ready to hear the depths of my insanity?"

"Stop," Gwen said, pulling away and giving Dante a serious look. "Just tell me whatever you can tell me. I want to help."

"I think it will be easier if I just get right to the point," Dante said, trying to gather his thoughts. "I don't remember much, well . . . other than this last time, but it's already fading."

"Then quit stalling," Gwen said, smiling this time.

"Touché," Dante said. "The headaches . . . they're bad, but I could deal with just them. I think . . . well, I know . . . each time, I get some picture, some . . . scene playing out in my head. It's like a memory, only . . . it's not."

"What do you mean?" Gwen asked.

"It's . . . it's so vivid. I feel like I'm there, like I've been there," Dante said. "But I haven't. I don't think anyone has. It just seems . . . impossible."

"Dante, I don't understand," Gwen said. "Been where?"

"This is the part that sounds crazy. Well, it all sounds crazy, but this is the craziest," Dante said. "Space. Somewhere in space. I've seen . . . I don't know . . . a planet that's not earth, but I've also seen earth, only from a distance. It's . . . I don't know. They start out so vivid, so real, but the longer I'm awake the more they fade, until I just feel . . . wrong."

Dante rested his head against his hands, leaning over and trying to remember details from the dream he'd just had. When he'd first awoken, it had seemed so real that he could have written a cheap science fiction novel with the details. As he sat there thinking, he could feel another headache rising. He held his breath for a second, hoping it would pass. With each headache, he worried more and more that he was losing his mind, possibly even his health.

"In the visions, I see . . . I . . . I see . . . the moon . . ." Dante paused, his head pounding as if something was trying to bore its way out. "I can't . . . death . . . the end . . ."

Dante's confession was interrupted by another vision. He slammed his hands onto the sides of his head and screamed. As he started to lose consciousness, he could see the look of fear on Gwen's face as his eyes once again rolled back, and he collapsed on the bed. His consciousness had already been ripped away from him by the time she leaped to the phone and quickly dialed 911. Within a few moments, the blaring sound of sirens broke through the usually quiet neighborhood and up the street. If he had been aware, Dante would have tried to stop Gwen from the call she immediately made, but he was so far gone this time that even the sensation of her lovingly holding his hand in the back of an ambulance meant nothing to him.

INTERLUDE

Laughter filled the cold, metallic ship as it soared majestically through the universe. The laughter, though, came only from one man. The man stood on a platform and looked at a gigantic three-dimensional map of the Milky Way Galaxy. For most of his life, he'd been nameless, but recently his plans had led him to a fateful interaction with a man who would know him as Ulysses, if his memory of their encounter hadn't been wiped clean. Regardless, Ulysses stuck to the shadows, in case Dante's visions became controllable at an advanced rate. His recent tests had proven inconclusive, but Ulysses could sense that Dante's mind was gathering occasional scattered images of him. If things went according to plan, then even should Dante catch a full glimpse of Ulysses, he'd only see him as an imposing figure with no identity.

Ulysses watched the floor below as a group of slightly larger than human creatures scurried about and performed their various tasks. Though the black, scaly creatures had great strength, in addition to sharp claws and teeth, Ulysses had proven himself dominant, though occasionally an alpha would try to rise above its station. Seemingly on cue, one of the larger creatures stopped, and used its pupilless eyes to shoot a threatening gaze towards Ulysses. It shot out its six-foot long tongue and licked its large, sharp teeth. Ulysses caught the glance and laughed loudly, with an unexpected, yet earned confidence. The creature dropped the heavy load it was carrying and leapt up three levels directly at Ulysses, who, still laughing, calmly reached out and grabbed the creature by the rough, cold black skin of its throat. He took hold of the creature's tongue, ripped it out and threw it over the ledge. The creatures below watched as the figure tightened his grip and lifted the creature's head off its body.

"Never forget your place here. Never forget who I am," said Ulysses, as he tossed the creature's head aside and walked out of the room, still laughing.

* * *

CHAPTER 14

JOHN

AFTER HE RECEIVED THE LATEST news on Dante's condition from Gwen, John Dawson, who had recently been promoted to field director, decided that it was time for him to take a more direct course of action. John, who had been an integral part of the CIA for more than 20 years, still considered Dante to be his best friend. That was the main reason he had remained uninvolved until absolutely necessary, even allowing Dante to take his chance at a normal life. Simply put, he knew his involvement, even if he managed to keep it under wraps for a while, would raise several flags and bring to light a few things that, for most, were better served being kept from public, or even government, scrutiny. John wiped his hands across his face, which had been aged both by time and by more crisis situations than he cared to count, and he pressed down softly on the intercom button.

"Janet, I need you to cancel all my appointments. There's a situation that needs my full attention. I'll be leaving immediately."

John looked down at his desk and picked up a picture frame. A few tears escaped from his dark blue, almost black, eyes, before he was able to quickly regain control of his emotions.

Well, Conner, you always said it was coming. I only wish you were alive to help me through what must be done. The only bright spot is that you helped to prepare in case it ever came down to this.

John sighed and took the back off of the frame, revealing a small envelope taped to the back of the picture. The envelope was about the size of a business card and had something written on the back. John sat and stared at the envelope for what, to him, seemed like an eternity of silent regret, and then once more at the picture. He sighed to himself and left the office, wondering if he would ever return again.

* * *

CHAPTER 15

DANTE

"WHERE . . . WHERE AM I?" ASKED Dante, finally regaining consciousness and not recognizing his sterile surroundings.

"Shhh. Don't over-exert yourself, honey. We're at the hospital," said Gwen. "You've been unconscious."

"How long?" Dante asked, being careful not to add the words 'this time.'

"About six hours," Gwen said, caressing his hair. "How do you feel?"

"I'm fine. We have to go. I've got to talk to John."

"Dante, you can't just leave the hospital. They have to run more tests on you. I want to know why all this is happening. Besides . . . I already called John. He'll be here."

"But . . . I need to leave. I promise I'll explain it to you. Will you please see if there's a way for me to get out of here?"

"Fine. I'll go ask around, but I'm not promising anything," Gwen said, kissing Dante on the forehead and walking out the door.

Dante knew that she was going to the cafeteria, and then would come back and tell him that there was nothing she could do. In fact, he counted on it, but he just needed some time to think. He knew that if he could just talk to John, they could figure everything out together. If there was anything to figure out, that is. The more this went on, the less sure of himself Dante became, to the point now that he somewhat even wished for it to all be a product of some type of insanity.

Still waiting for Gwen to return, he thought about the times that John and he had been in life-threatening situations. When Dante was working his way through Princeton, it was John who was ever present as a friend. At the time, Dante hadn't known that John was in the CIA, or how that would impact his own life. After Dante graduated from Princeton with honors and degrees in Political Science and Biochemistry, and a minor in theatre he'd completed on a dare, John introduced him to his niece,

Gwendolyn Watson, and used his influence from years of experience in the CIA to get Dante a position with the CIA. Through hard work and an excellent case record, Dante quickly became one of the preeminent agents within the ranks, serving with John as his handler.

Though it had only been a few weeks since Dante had issued his resignation from the CIA, despite John's disappointment, it felt as if it had been a lifetime ago. Even though he hated hurting John's feelings, he felt that was the only way to give his wife a normal life. For him, right now, even with the pain still creeping through his temples, Gwen was his main concern. He remembered the butterflies he felt on their first date, a sensation that had never happened to him before . . .

* * *

INTERLUDE

"Yes, John . . . I'm pulling up in front of her apartment right now . . . I promise, best behavior. Right, right . . . whoops . . . losing service . . ."

Dante laughed to himself as he slammed the phone shut in the midst of John's almost-parental-like ramblings on first date behavior. As he reached for the handle to his 2004 Thunderbird, which admittedly had seen better days, he reopened the phone and turned it completely off, just to be safe. The last thing he wanted was to have to explain why to Gwen why her uncle was calling him every five minutes. It had been months, or maybe even years, since Dante had gone on anything even resembling a date, so he felt a strong mixture of nervousness and excitement building up as he walked up the concrete path to Gwen's door. When the door slowly crept open, Dante was momentarily speechless. The feelings of nervousness and excitement were gone, replaced with something else . . . something he'd never felt before. Not love, he wasn't a believer in love at first sight, but there was something special, something he couldn't even describe.

"You're right on time! Let me grab my purse and wave off my roommate." Gwen said, her blue dress bringing out the brightness of her eyes.

On the outside, Dante smiled back and nodded his understanding, while inside he cursed at himself for not having anything charming or funny to say. *Even hello probably would have been a step up.* When Gwen returned, Dante silently led her to his car, making sure to open the door for her. If the entire date was going to turn him into a strangely out of place character from an old silent movie, at least he was going to be a strange but POLITE character.

"John's told me a lot about you, but one thing really stands out . . . I've got to ask . . . theatre?" Gwen seemingly stifled a laugh.

Clearing his throat quietly, Dante was finally able to feel the ability to speak reappear, so he attempted a sincere answer.

"Dare," he said, blinking quickly at the vagueness of his own response. "It was a dare from my roommate. He was making fun of how little sense it made to study Political Science and Biochemistry, and one thing led to another . . . and he dared me to try and find a minor even farther away from science, so . . . I did."

With that first admission out of the way, Dante finally felt he was in control of himself enough to make somewhat of a positive impression on the date. The rest of the night flew by, although Gwen definitely carried more of the conversation. However, Dante soon realized it was more because he longed to hear what she had to say and not so much because he was tongue tied. When it finally came time for Dante to walk Gwen back to her apartment door, he was sure beyond a shadow of a doubt there was no one else he wanted to be dating.

"I've got to admit . . . I'm not a fan of setups from my uncle," Gwen said, fishing the keys out of her purse. "But you passed, Dante Smith. Congratulations."

Dante had to laugh, "Well, thank you. John's description of you didn't come close to doing you justice."

"Call me, I'd love to go out again," Gwen smiled and unlocked her door. "By the way, I don't kiss on the first date, so don't take this as a sign."

Dante was floored by the directness and honesty, and once again felt that speechlessness from earlier in the night. Still, he managed to fight it off long enough to smile and nod and throw out a random, "I'll call ya."

For the first time in a long time, everything in Dante's life felt right.

CHAPTER 16

DANTE

"WHAT'S WRONG? IS IT HAPPENING again?" said Gwen, appearing at the door.

"No . . . not this time. I was just reminiscing. Well . . . what's the verdict?"

"They want you to stay in for observation. Sorry . . . I tried," Gwen said, avoiding eye contact.

Dante smiled and pulled her close to kiss her. He knew that he would get out soon, and he didn't really see the point in arguing over it now. When Dante reached to kiss Gwen again, she pulled away with a strange look on her face.

"Dante, I want to know what is happening. You were about to say something earlier . . . before this . . . something about the moon. What was it?"

The smile on Dante's face was immediately replaced with a serious, pained expression. He shut his eyes, rubbed his hands across his goatee and swallowed.

"I'm not crazy. I wasn't sure of that until a few minutes ago, but I'm not. This is going to sound crazy, but you have to believe me. I can't explain everything. I don't know why I'm having these . . . seizures . . . but I do know that I'm having visions. The visions are so intense and horrifying . . . so . . . horrible. I'm not sure you should have to be a part of this."

"That's not your choice to make. I knew you were different from the first time I met you. The only thing that changed when you quit the FBI was your job. You have always been the same man with the same worries and problems," Gwen sat down on the edge of the bed and softly caressed Dante's hand. "I made a promise to be with you for better or worse, so spill it"

"I guess you're right. You do have a right to know. Over the past few weeks, I've been having incredibly realistic dreams . . . visions, I guess, of . . . of the future? Yeah, it has to be the future. Everything is destroyed. I see piles of bodies being burned in the street. I see toppled buildings and explosions filling the air and the streets. Those are always the constants, but the past few have been slightly different. I've seen more."

"No wonder you've been acting so different lately. The strain of seeing all that death . . . all that destruction . . . it's no wonder you wound up in the hospital," Gwen interrupted.

"That's not all. In the last two, I haven't just seen, but I've heard, too . . . heard a voice. I don't know who it belongs to, but I know that it is speaking to me, warning me . . . no . . . threatening me. In the last vision, I almost saw the face of the person it belongs to, but he wouldn't step out of the shadows. I saw him kill, though. He murdered a . . . a creature of some type, an alien, maybe, in cold blood."

Dante sat silently for a moment, holding Gwen close and wondering what was going through her mind. He could remember when the headaches started, and if he really focused, he could even remember parts of his first vision, but he had no idea what was causing them. Despite the danger of his last mission with the CIA, Dante wondered if he'd made the right decision in resigning. If he'd stayed, then maybe John and the higher ups could have fixed things before they were completely broken.

"That, my friend, is why we must leave immediately," came a voice from the doorway.

Dante and Gwen both turned to see who had walked in and interrupted. Gwen stood up and rushed to the figure in the doorway and threw her arms around him.

"John! Thank you so much for coming. I know you're busy, but . . ." Gwen said.

"I didn't come just because you requested me, Gwendolyn. I came because Dante's entire life has built to this moment . . . to what is coming," John said. "I've filed the appropriate paper work, Dante. You are free to leave this place and come with me. We have a lot to do."

"What are you talking about? You seem to know an awful lot more about this than I do. What's going on?" Dante said.

"I'll explain it all soon. Now, hurry and dress. We can't waste any more time than we already have. I have something I must retrieve from a . . . from a nearby base. Take Gwen home and wait for me there."

Dante nodded his head as John walked out of the room. Gwen and Dante exchanged a worried glance, before Dante slowly rolled out of bed and walked to the shelf that held his clothes. As good as it was to see John, unfortunately his arrival meant that everything he'd experienced was at the very least something he needed to worry about . . . and very possibly something much, much worse.

CHAPTER 17

DANTE

DANTE OPENED THE DOOR TO his closet, still not sure what he was about to do. It had taken them less than half an hour to leave the hospital and arrive home, but it had seemed longer as John's impending arrival hung over the silence between he and Gwen. Dante, in an attempt to pass the time until John arrived, carefully went through a small drawer in the very back of the closet. The door had not been opened for years, other than a quick addition just after his resignation, and Dante had hoped never to look in it again. He pulled out a small necklace with a golden spider on it and stared at it. It had been a wedding gift from John, mostly meant as a joke. Dante had always been terrified of any kind of spider, but held a strange admiration for Spider-Man, largely because of his hero's overwhelming sense of responsibility and desire to protect his loved ones . . . something he and Dante had in common; John never failed to point out the irony in the situation. He smiled and put the necklace around his neck and tucked it into his plain black T-shirt.

The next thing he came across in the drawer was a revolver and holster, which he attached to his shirt. He hadn't held a gun since his last mission, but in a flash, everything came burning back into his memory. All the missions, all the nearly impossible scenarios . . . everything he'd gone through in his old life was still there. Really, it would never leave him, no matter how much he occasionally wished it would. Then, out of the corner of his eye, Dante noticed a box in the corner marked 'junk.' He closed the drawer and opened the box. Going through the box he came across an old Cincinnati Reds baseball jersey, buried beneath the piles of batteries, old papers, never-read books, and other items that had outlived their usefulness. He remembered buying it during his freshman year of college and wearing it about twice a week or more throughout his college years. He picked it up out of the box, smiled, shook all the wrinkles out of it, and carefully put it on.

"I can't believe you found that thing. I remember you used to do everything but bathe in that thing," Gwen said from the doorway.

"Hey, it's my lucky shirt, and I think I'm going to need some luck now," Dante said, walking over to his wife. "Besides, I think we all know that secretly, you chose me because of this shirt."

Gwen laughed and reached up to kiss her husband, "I think you mean 'in spite of that shirt,' but don't be getting any ideas now. John's here. He's downstairs in the living room with a briefcase, and he doesn't look very calm."

"Well, I'd better not keep him waiting any more then, princess," Dante said, kissing his wife. "I want to find out what he knows about all of this, and why it's happening to me in the first place."

Dante held Gwen close for a moment, and then turned around and left the room. As he walked down the stairs, he could hear John talking on the phone. He stopped just before he entered the living room and listened to John's end of the conversation. He couldn't make out much, but did notice his name being mentioned. Dante cleared his throat, in order to let John know he was standing there, and walked into the room. John quickly hung up the phone and sat down across from Dante at a small table in the center of the room.

"Well, John, I'm pretty sure you weren't ordering a pizza . . . so what was that phone call about?"

"I was discussing our current situation with . . . a friend. The call, however, is not something we need to discuss . . . yet," John said. "Right now, you need to tell me exactly what's been happening so that I can figure out how far along we are."

"What do you mean 'how far along we are?' What are you talking about? I think you need to tell me what you know, and don't leave anything out."

"Very well, if you would rather hear my end of the story first, that's fine. You won't like what you hear, though," John said, opening his briefcase and pulling out a file. "Before I tell you what I know, you need to look over this."

Dante took the file. It was marked 'Top Secret—Highest Security Clearance.' He looked up at John, who matched Dante's questioning glance with a nod and a deep sigh. Dante slowly opened the file and read over the first page. It was a summary of a secret NASA mission that involved Dante's father, Conner Smith. Dante remembered his dad telling him about his short stint as an astronaut, but he had never mentioned anything about this. Dante decided to save all his questions for the end, because he had a bad feeling that he would have a lot more. His misgivings were unfortunately proven right with the next page. He rubbed his eyes in disbelief as he gazed upon a photograph of one of the creatures he had seen in his last vision. The only difference was that it was much smaller, perhaps an indication of its age. The next page revealed a picture of a large space ship. It was rounded and spherical in the front, but eventually gave way to straight lines and a strange triangle shaped tail. He had never seen a ship like this before, but the markings showed it was a NASA designed craft. The final few pages focused on Dante himself. According to the paperwork, he wasn't as normal as he had always believed. He closed the file and shot a desperate glance towards John for answers.

"John, what's going on? That . . . thing . . . I saw one in one of my visions . . . what is it? Where did it come from? How does my father's mission fit into all this?"

"I'm afraid if I tell you all of the answers you seek, then you may never have a normal life again. There is no way you can escape what will happen once you know everything." John said cryptically.

"Do you think I have a normal life right now? I live every day afraid that one of these seizures that accompany after the visions will end my life and leave Gwen alone. I want to know. No, I need to know everything."

"Then you will. First, I want you to forget every rumor and all the misinformed prattle about Area 51 and aliens landing on Earth. That 'creature' you saw in the picture . . . it didn't land here . . . so to speak," John paused, noticeably shaken. "Shortly before your birth, 10 months to be exact, your father, Conner, took part in a top secret mission for NASA to test a new spacecraft with warping technology. No one, other than those directly involved, knew anything about this. We didn't even explain everything to the two astronauts; your father and a young woman named Greta Williams. They were to fly the spacecraft just past the moon, engage the warping technology, and immediately return."

"Warping technology? What kind of warping technology?" Dante asked.

"Contrary to popular scientific belief, we had developed a way to travel faster than the speed of light. There was a device built into the spacecraft that had the ability to open a small rift in space, a warp zone, and then close it again after the craft went through. Using this technology, the spacecraft could travel nearly anywhere in the universe without the threat of time," John stopped again and wiped his hands across his eyes. "However, during the test run, we lost contact with the ship for hours. We were about to declare the mission a failure and notify the families of the astronauts, when the warp zone reopened in the same place, and the spacecraft shot though."

"My father . . . he almost died testing some stupid technology that you don't even use now? Did Greta live through it? What about the alien? Did it return with them?"

"Your father . . . he was a hero. Yes, Greta did live through the mission, but unfortunately not long afterwards. As for the alien, it did return with them, but not in the manner you have surmised. When we reached the spacecraft, both astronauts were unconscious but, physically, in the same shape as before, except we found that Greta was pregnant." John placed his hand on Dante's shoulder, but it was immediately brushed off. "She wasn't pregnant when she went up, so we knew that it couldn't have been Conner's child. In a matter of weeks, she gave birth to the 'creature' you saw in the picture. Neither of them lived through childbirth, but the creature's body continued to grow despite its death. We ran every test imaginable on your father and found nothing amiss. As far as we knew, he was completely normal."

"As far as you knew? You sent him home knowing there could be a chance of something happening to him? What about my mother's safety? What if she had given birth to one of those . . . oh God. Earlier, you . . . you said this took place 10 months before I was born. Why did you point that out?" Dante stood up quickly and grabbed John by his coat.

"When you were born, you were physically normal, at least as far as outward appearances went. We arranged for samples of your blood and DNA to be taken without the knowledge of your parents or any of the doctors. We found a strange strand of DNA in your genetic code. There was nothing we could do about it, and it didn't appear to be causing you any ill effects. In fact, as you grew, it did quite the opposite," John said, calmly removing himself from Dante's grip and walking across the room. "During your recent stay at the hospital, we found that your DNA had changed again slightly. I believe that it is somehow related to your visions over the past few weeks."

Dante caught John's arm as he was walking away, "What you're saying . . . it means . . . I'm not . . . I'm not normal. How could you let me live my life thinking that I had any chance of being normal? That means . . . the visions . . . the voice I heard . . . they're real. Everything is going to end . . . everyone is going to die . . ."

"Not necessarily. We had no idea when this day would come, or even if it would come, but many people, including myself, have spent their entire lives preparing for it. No spacecraft have arrived in our vicinity as of yet, but that means we must hurry. There is more I need to tell you, more to prepare you for, but this isn't the place. I have to return these files to my friend at NASA, but after that I'm flying to our base in New Mexico. Area 51."

"I thought you told me to forget everything I've heard about 'Area 51.' Was that a lie, too?" Dante said.

"No, it wasn't a lie. Yes, there is an Area 51 . . . but there are no aliens there. We use it as both a fallback base, and as a place to test new weapons and spacecraft. Everything is below ground and completely undetectable. The 'Area 51' of myths—the sterile, secretive military base surrounded with top security—is simply a cover. Nothing important happens at that base, but if we provide a place for people to question, then they are less likely to go looking for one," John said. "You have to come with me, Dante. The only way for you to find your answers . . . and for us to get through the upcoming disaster . . . is for you to come with me. I will arrange for a car to pick you up in half an hour to take you to the airport."

"Wait . . . John . . . what am I? I need to know . . . if my life is a lie . . . if everything I've ever accomplished was a lie . . . if our friendship was a lie."

John paused, "Dante . . . I truly am sorry. While it is true that I first made contact with you as a way to keep track of you, our friendship is real. I look at you as a son . . . and that's why I never told you before. I didn't want to shake up your life just because of a situation that might never happen. We'll get through this . . . son. I'll see you at the airport, and we will go get the answers together."

Dante nodded and shook John's hand. He watched as John walked out of the house and entered his car. Rubbing his hand over his face, he remembered Gwen and how he had to tell her something, but was afraid to tell her everything. He walked up the stairs and found Gwen still in the bedroom cleaning the closet. He went over to her and held her close. She looked at him with a concerned look and instinctively went to sit on the bed.

“What’s wrong, Dante? What did John tell you? Is this all going to be over soon?” Gwen asked, barely holding back the tears.

“There is a lot more to this than what I thought, Gwen. It involves something that happened to my father a long time ago . . . when he was still an astronaut. I still don’t know everything, but I will soon. I’m going to go to New Mexico with John . . . to a military base . . . and I should find all the answers there,” Dante said. “I want you to go to Tampa and stay with your parents until I get back, okay?”

“Dante, I know you’re not telling me everything. I’ll accept that for now, but why do I have to leave? Why does John need you and not someone else? You haven’t been in the FBI for years . . .”

“Honey, I can’t tell you everything . . . not yet . . . it’s not safe. You have to stay with your parents, because I don’t want to have to worry about you being alone while I’m gone,” Dante said, slowly caressing Gwen’s hair with one hand and holding her hand with the other. “This isn’t about my being in the FBI . . . it’s about me. I have to find out . . . I have to get some things answered. I promise that everything will be okay soon.”

Gwen nodded and Dante pulled her close. The two sat holding each other until a car arrived in front of the house to take Dante to the airport. After a tearful goodbye, and a renewed promise that Gwen would go to her parents’ house, Dante stepped into the car to be ushered closer to his destiny.

CHAPTER 18

JOHN

FROM THE MOMENT JOHN LEFT Dante's home to the moment he finished his errands, he could do nothing but wonder how much better he could have handled this entire situation. He'd always hated the way people clung to the idea of "destiny," but he couldn't shake the first time he'd truly met Dante. Perhaps if he'd handled things better then, he wouldn't have to completely destroy the life he'd built for himself now.

INTERLUDE

"Destiny. It is a word that gets thrown around much more than need be, simply because it sounds important. Next slide. I'm here to tell you, seniors, that your destiny is what you make it, and I don't mean that simply as a cliché or a recruiting pitch, mostly because the CIA is very selective, and we don't really need to recruit."

John paused, waiting for the sound of laughter to punch through the awkward silence that had hung over most of his speech. He absolutely hated going to high schools to speak, and he especially hated being at this one. It had been years since Conner died, and the last thing he wanted to do was raise too many questions or suspicions in the mind of his son. Still, John knew that it was past time to make contact and check on his progress.

"Thank you for your time. I consider it an honor to be permitted to speak before all of the impressive seniors contending for an academic honors diploma. I wish you the best of luck in all your future endeavors," John said, partially wishing he had stopped talking about twenty minutes ago.

"Thank you, Agent Dawson. Class, please give Agent Dawson a round of applause for taking the time from his busy schedule to speak with us," the teacher said, leading the class in a sputtering of applause. "Does anyone have any questions for Agent Dawson before the bell rings?"

John stifled the urge to roll his eyes, not expecting much in the way of intelligent questions. Regardless of how smart the students in this room were, he knew he'd been boring, a fact in which he actually took great pride. The more boring his job sounded, the less he had to lie when it came to answering questions involving matters of national security.

"I have a question . . . are you the Agent Dawson that led the cover-up on Conner Smith's death?"

John's throat suddenly felt very dry. He'd expected a few alien questions, but he'd assumed Dante would have no knowledge of anything involving his father's death or previous activities. *Did Conner tell him everything . . . or has Dante stumbled across some files that should have been destroyed.*

"Dante! Agent Dawson is a guest here, I will not have you rudely . . ."

"It's okay, ma'am," John cut off the teacher, not wanting to add to Dante's suspicion by allowing him to get in trouble for an honest question. "May I ask your name, son?"

John audibly gasped as Dante stood up. Even at age eighteen, the boy was every bit his father's son. John wondered what else they had in common, or how much Conner's "secret" past would affect Dante's life and development.

"I believe you know my name, sir, but I'll play along. Dante Smith. 18. Son of Conner Smith, former astronaut, although strangely, most records of his missions seem to be missing from public record. Key word, sir: most."

"Well, son, I believe you have me all wrong," John hoped Dante hadn't progressed far enough to detect any subtle stretching of the truth. "Your father and I were actually very close, and we even worked together on a few of those missions to which you've referred. However, to my knowledge, there's been no "secret government cover-up," but rather just certain missions regarded as Top Secret. Honestly, son, it's a sign of how important your father's contribution to . . ."

"Sir, with all due respect, spare me the company line. I've spent most of my life getting the runaround when it comes to any and all questions I have about my father. And, if you'd be so kind . . . don't call me son. The only man that can call me son is dead, as I'm sure you well know."

"Dante . . . I don't think you . . ." John was torn between protecting the mission, as he'd always done, and reaching out to the only thing left of one of his closest friends.

"That will be quite enough, Dante. Agent Dawson, I apologize on behalf of Dante and the rest of the class," the teacher's timely response merely delayed John's inevitable decision. "Class, you are all dismissed . . . except you, Dante."

John kept his gaze on Dante, retaking his seat angrily, as the rest of the class filed by, some taking the time to shake his hand, others simply passing by as if nothing had happened. As John watched the teacher attempt to explain to Dante how respect works, he made a simple decision. Both for his and Dante's sake, if he took this moment to step in and share something, anything at all, then he may be able to forge the beginning of a relationship that would ease Dante's suspicions, while allowing John to keep a closer eye on how everything progressed.

"Excuse me, ma'am, but I'd like to have a private word with young Dante here, regarding his father."

John stepped in, placing a calming hand on the teacher's shoulder, with just enough force to let her know he was quite capable of taking care of things on his own. In order to survive over the years, John had learned to read people quite well, and he knew that she was debating the consequences of letting one of her students go off with a man from the government, both for his and her own safety.

"I'm an old friend of his fathers, and I believe I can clear a few things up . . . save us all some embarrassment down the line," John said with a smile.

Finally, the teacher nodded her approval and went back to her desk. John wasn't sure if he'd convinced her with his smile, or if she simply had an irrational fear of the government and just wanted the day to end without any arrests. With the public part of the interaction out of the way, John was positive he could professionally handle everything from here on out. After all, he'd made a promise to Conner years ago that, should the day come he was in danger, John would do everything in his power to train and protect Dante, even at the cost of his own life. It was a promise he had every intention of keeping. Once they were outside the school, but still in line of sight with a few security cameras to ensure John would appear as a friendly aide and not as a strong-armed government militant picking on a lowly high school senior, John began his tale.

"Even though you could have handled it better, I admit, if I were in your place, I'd be filled with questions, as well," John said. "Everything I said in there was true, Dante. The only missions not a part of public record were part of a special training program or equipment testing mission. Nothing that led to your father's death, I assure you."

"Why would I take your word on that? If you're part of a cover-up, it's obvious you'd play me with half-truths and misdirection."

John was both impressed and annoyed at how on top of things Dante seemed to be in this case. This was definitely something he had to wrap up quickly, because the longer this conversation went, the more of a chance for Dante to poke holes in everything he was about to hear.

"Your father and I were very close. In fact, he made me promise to take care of you should he ever pass on before me. Unfortunately . . . I just couldn't, Dante," John knew to stick to half-truths and emotional responses, as even an advanced 18 year old was still a teenager without a father. "When your father passed, and I saw you at the funeral . . . a four year old boy with no father . . . every part of me wanted to step in and fulfill my promise . . ."

John paused, partially to sell the story, and partially because he truly did feel a welling up of emotion at his failure to give Dante some of what he missed by losing his father at such an early age.

"I was a much younger man, then, and I just couldn't imagine being good enough to fill Conner's shoes. Your mother didn't really know me and had no reason to trust me, and I feared that with all of my time away in the CIA, I'd do more harm than good. I'm truly sorry, Dante," John said.

"Mom and I were fine. My issue isn't with you not raising me, Agent Dawson . . . John. It's with all the questions surrounding my father's death. Why can't I know . . . why can't mom know . . . why is everything so secret?" Dante said, seeming to barely hold himself together.

"I truly wish I could tell you everything, s . . . Dante, but I simply don't have the clearance. I can honestly tell you this, though, your father was a true hero, and there is no cover-up about his death. Everyone that's ever heard of him understands and respects his sacrifice, and no one would want to rob you of information about his unfortunate and untimely death," John knew he was being watched, so it was high time to wrap this up. "The secrecy is simply because of the equipment being tested . . . equipment that was purely for the good of mankind. There is no connection to his death. Please . . . if you believe anything I say, believe that."

John hoped against all odds that he'd pulled this off, and that Dante would buy at least enough of what he'd said to put away his apparent crusade. For a moment, he wasn't sure if Dante was going to reply at all, as he simply stared down at his feet, more than likely collecting his thoughts and processing everything that had happened today.

"I . . . I don't entirely believe you . . . but what you said, it mostly sounds true," Dante said. "At the very least, I'll go ahead and buy that you're being sincere. Anyway, I really need to get home and make sure mom's okay. I appreciate your time, Agent Dawson."

"It's John. Call me John," John said, handing Dante his business card. "I know you've got more questions, and I'll do my best to help you with them. I may have ruined my chance to completely honor Conner's wishes, but please contact me if you need anything in the future. You never know . . . maybe one day, we'll even work a mission together."

John and Dante shared a slightly nervous laugh, but John could tell that a once volatile situation had calmed down considerably. Perhaps through an initial frightening moment in public, John had even managed to set a foundation that would enable everything to eventually work out for the best in the future.

INTERLUDE

The sky of the small, but densely populated, planet turned black as the immense metallic vessel entered the atmosphere. Crowds of the unnamed planet's gangly, orange and white inhabitants ran out of their hut-like homes and looked up at the seemingly shapeless spaceship. The spacecraft was spherical on one end, but its rounded edges gave way to straight lines and an indescribable triangle-like tail. Some of the planet's older inhabitants began to bow and send their praises up to the craft.

On board the ship, the black, scaly creatures hustled back and forth preparing the teleportation area. Ulysses stood silently, watching his minions scurry about. He walked towards one of the creatures that was typing instructions into the teleportation console and grabbed it by the arm.

"I want the inhabitants of this planet obliterated quickly. This is our final step of preparation before we engage the warp engine and move to the Earth's galaxy." The figure tightened his grip and lifted the creature up by its arm, "There is no room for failure. Send the invasion force down now."

Ulysses released his grip and walked down a small corridor to his chambers, shutting the door behind him. A loud clicking noise emanated from the creature's throat, and thousands of his brethren answered the call and stepped by pairs into the teleportation chamber. The creature flipped a switch on the console and watched the events below on a large three-dimensional area in the center of the room. The invasion was quick and ruthless, sped along because of the peaceful and trusting nature of the planet's inhabitants. Mere minutes after the creatures entered the portal, they returned victorious. Laughter was heard from the figure's chamber as the scans for life showed that there was none remaining.

* * *

CHAPTER 19

GWEN

GWEN WATCHED FROM THE DOORWAY for several minutes after the car carrying Dante pulled away from the house. She didn't understand everything that was going on, and she knew that Dante hadn't told her everything. She understood that he was just being protective, though. In fact she was doing the same thing for him, in a way. She closed the door and walked softly towards the bathroom. She silently picked up the small plastic pregnancy test out of the trash and looked at it intently.

"I can't believe it came out positive. Dante, please hurry back. I need you."

CHAPTER 20

JOHN

"WELL, DANTE, I TRUST THE car ride was to your satisfaction?" John said, extending his hand.

"It was fine. Let's get going, John. I want to get this behind me as soon as I can," Dante walked past John's extended hand and seated himself near the back of the plane.

John dropped his head and slowly walked to the cockpit to discuss something with the pilot. Dante didn't want things to be like this between him and John, but at the moment he didn't see how they could be any different. He had just left his wife and his life in Miami to fly across the country to try to stop something that he didn't even fully understand. He watched John move to the back of the plane and sit down next to him as the plane began to take off.

"John, what's going to happen to me? You told me that I have different DNA than normal people, but what exactly does that mean?"

John turned and looked at Dante without answering, and then looked away.

"John? I'm leaving my wife . . . my life . . . behind, because you told me I wasn't normal and because you said I was the only possible way out of this. The least you can do is respond to me when I talk to you."

"I don't know, son. I don't have all the answers. That is what this trip is about. There is something at the base that will answer more questions than you probably even want answered. Just be patient."

More than anything, Dante hated the feeling of being unable to trust John. Granted it wasn't the first time he'd felt that way, but it had been years since they met, and he felt John had more than proven himself in that time. Still, this was HIS life being torn apart, not John's, so Dante felt he was entitled to know everything he was about to face and why.

"Patient. I'm supposed to be patient. I can't believe that I honestly thought you would give me a straight answer. I can't believe . . . I . . ." Dante clutched his head and screamed. The last thing he saw before losing consciousness was the shock and horror on the face of his friend.

* * *

INTERLUDE

"Plans have been altered. I see that our course has taken us near the planet Ambur. Set the transport for one more test run before we head to the Earth's galaxy," said the booming voice of Ulysses, still hidden by shadows. "They have weaponry similar to that of Earth, and it will prove interesting to see how it fares against our attack."

Ulysses watched silently as the scaly black creature flipped a switch and then made a loud clicking noise. Without hesitation, most of the rest of the spacecraft's inhabitants lined up and, without any questions, marched through the transport area. Ulysses turned his attention away from the creature working the transport controls and reached out to turn on the three-dimensional monitor. On the screen, a small militia of armed pink skinned, wolf-like creatures surrounded a few of the creatures he had sent forth. Ulysses watched as his warriors marched through a barrage of projectile fire and, although many were hit, showed no signs of harm. Seemingly satisfied, Ulysses turned off the monitor and walked back to his private room.

CHAPTER 21

DANTE

Dante awoke with a loud gasp and sat straight up. He looked around at the small, empty room he was lying in and slowly began to remember boarding the plane and having another vision. Getting out of the small, sheetless bed, he saw that there were no visible doors. He walked around the small room, rubbing his hand along each wall trying to discern a way out. Just before he once again reached the bed, he felt an odd tingle and jumped back as his hand went through the wall. Realizing that some sort of advanced holographic technology was being used, he took a deep breath and stepped through.

"Well, Dante, it's good to see you up and around. I see that it didn't take long for you to find a way out of your quarters," John said from a large wall of monitors and controls.

"I get the feeling that I was just in some kind of test, John, and I don't like that. If you want to test me, then you come to me and tell me that. Don't set up little surprises for me when I'm waking up from a vision."

"Well, it wasn't entirely a test. This level of the base doesn't use doors, because they can be . . . too inviting. I will inform you of any future needs to test you, though," John placed his hand on Dante's shoulder. "We need to get things started immediately. I need you to tell me everything you can about the visions as we head to the lower lab."

Dante nodded his head and walked out of the computer room with John. For a while, the two were silent and Dante did nothing but think of his wife at home. He felt some sort of sense of urgency when he thought about her, and he didn't like that. Arriving at what could only be described as an elevator, Dante and John began their descent into the recesses of the base.

"I told you earlier about some of the visions, and I know you overheard me telling Gwen about the voice I heard in the one right before the hospital."

"Yes, that's true. You have had one since then, though. It is imperative that you tell me about it. It might give us some clue as to how much time we have."

Dante shot John a quizzical stare, but continued speaking anyway, "I heard the voice again. I couldn't see his face, though. He made sure to stay only in areas where the shadows were prevalent. For a second, I could see with his eyes . . . I could see what was happening on the planet his creatures were invading. The planet's inhabitants . . . they fought back . . . they shot them . . . but nothing could stop their advance. What's worse is . . . I feel that was their last stop before they come here."

John closed his eyes and bowed his head, and the two remained silent until the elevator reached the bottom level and the doors opened. John stepped out ahead of Dante and walked up to a small monitor on the other side of the very small room. Dante stepped out into a small room, about 12 ft. by 12 ft. and a ceiling that barely hung a foot above his head.

"What's going on, John? There's nothing down here."

John was looking intently at the monitor and pressing a few buttons on the small control panel just beneath it.

"You're wrong. This place isn't nothing, it's everything," John pushed another series of buttons and the monitor flashed to life, and a small, hand-shaped screen appeared just below the buttons. "Dante, this is just the doorway. The lock is set to be open only by you. I've set it up, now you just need to step over here and place your hand on the screen below the buttons so it can check your fingerprints."

Dante nodded his head and placed his hand on the designated screen. Upon contact, the monitor flashed again and another mechanism appeared next to it. The monitor was now asking for his visual patterns, so he stepped up to the new mechanism and placed his eye in front of it. After a few seconds, he heard a small clicking noise, followed by a series of low-pitched beeps. The monitor flashed a final time, and Dante could read his name on the screen. John pulled Dante away from the mechanisms and the monitor disappeared into the wall. For a moment, there were no noises or motion from anywhere. Dante looked over at John for answers, but he seemed to be just as intrigued by the events taking place. Finally, after nearly a minute, the entire wall began to shake and a small doorway appeared in the center. Dante and John turned to each other, shrugged, and proceeded through the doorway. Dante could tell that the new room was much larger, but there was no light except that which came through the doorway.

"John, where are we? Is it supposed to be so dark in here?"

John didn't have time to answer the question before the wall began shaking again and the doorway shut behind them. The room stayed dark for an instant. The lights came on slowly, allowing the two the time necessary to get used to a new source of light. The room itself was slightly larger than an average room, about 40 square feet, and was nearly empty. The only things that Dante could see were a table in the center with some sort of box taking up its full length, and another keypad on the far wall. Dante walked directly to the box on the table and tried to open it, before realizing that it was locked. He turned and gave John a look, which could best be described as a mixture of confusion and hope. John pulled a small, square envelope out of his pocket and handed it to Dante. The envelope was about the size of a business card and appeared to be fairly old. Dante closely examined the envelope. It was labeled, 'Keep him safe' and was signed by Conner Smith, his father. He glanced at John, who turned his head away for a second and then motioned towards the chest on the table. Dante nodded and quickly opened the envelope, which was empty except for two small keys, a silver one and a golden one. He focused on the chest. The only lock he could see was silver, so he took the silver key and turned it slowly in the lock. The lock clicked and the lid to the chest sprang open, revealing a small cassette recorder with a tape in it, three pictures of Conner, and a series of papers with Conner's handwriting on them. Dante picked up the tape recorder and hit play, rightfully expecting to hear his father's voice but still not prepared.

Conner Smith's voice started slow and shakily, but eventually became the strong voice that Dante remembered from his youth, "Dante, if you are hearing this . . . then the moment that we all hoped . . . prayed . . . would never take place is about to happen. Son, I want you to know that I wish that there were some way to keep you from being involved in this, but thanks to what happened on my mission . . . there's not. I suppose that by now John has told you, or arranged for you to find out, about most of the details of my mission, including what happened to Greta and that creature she gave birth to. What you don't know, however, is what happened during the time after we entered the warp zone and the time we returned. As much as I wish there was another way, I feel the best way for you to truly understand is to experience it . . . in a manner of speaking."

Before Dante could even react to what the image of his long-dead father was saying, he felt quick jolt, slightly similar to his visions, but not nearly as painful, and then everything went black.

* * *

INTERLUDE

"ALL SYSTEMS CHECK OUT, WILLIAMS. Prep the warp tech."

"Consider it prepped, Conner. By the way, considering our lives could end at any point on this mission, don't you think you can try to call me Greta?"

Conner flipped a switch to begin the preliminary countdown to warp, and then turned to his partner, making sure to give her his most serious and professional look.

"I'm sorry, Williams, I'm just used to working with men. Old habits die hard. I'll do my best, though," Conner said, watching the numbers count down and bracing himself, even though there were still minutes to spare. "How are you holding up? I know I miss Becky something fierce, and I know you just getting engaged . . ."

Greta cut him off, "Conner, I love that you're finally opening up a little, but I don't think this is quite the time. Return trip, we'll swap sob stories, okay?"

Conner laughed, "Deal, kiddo. Deal."

With just a few seconds left, Conner sighed and pictured his wife, hoping against all odds he'd get the chance to be with her again, to start the family she so desperately wanted. Once the clock hit zero, Conner and Greta simultaneously pressed the flashing orange buttons that popped up in front of each of them, and then were met with a near-deafening whistle that hopefully meant the mostly-untested warp technology was working. After the whistle came complete and total silence for a brief moment, though when telling the story at home, Conner would swear it felt like hours.

Before he had a chance to check their new coordinates versus their previous location, everything on the ship went black and stopped.

"Conner . . . what's . . ."

Another loud whistle interrupted Greta and startled Conner enough to the point that he actually felt afraid for the first time on a mission. The sudden sideways lurching of the ship did nothing to calm his fears, and, as light finally returned to the ship, and he was able to see outside, he knew that nothing would ever be the same again.

"Williams, that's . . . is that a spaceship?"

Conner's question was met with silence, though he would have ignored any reply, simply because he couldn't draw his attention away from the massive metallic object slowly and methodically drawing them towards it. Obviously the subject of possible extraterrestrial life and even contact had come up during their training, but Conner never truly believed it was something he'd have to face. At the most, he thought he'd find signs of life from generations past, or maybe even another planets' prehistoric beginnings, but he was about to literally come face to face with proof of life elsewhere in the universe. Despite some slight pangs of scientific curiosity, he mostly felt apprehension, and fear that he and Becky would never get to start that family.

After a few seconds, their unplanned journey reached its final destination, and the airlock doors sprung open. Conner shuddered at the scream which escaped Greta upon the entrance of the alien inhabitants of the ship. Their black scaly skin and dark pupilless eyes gave the appearance of a viciousness unlike anything Conner had ever experienced, and when they attempted to speak, their sharp teeth and long tongues spoke volumes more than their incomprehensible clicking noises. Conner feared the worst, and prepared himself to defend Greta, but, at least for now, it seemed things may not be all they appeared. Though he still couldn't make heads nor tails of their clicking, they gently led him and Greta out of their ship and aboard the alien craft. Before he could protest at being taken to a different part of the ship, though, all of the bright colors and odd shapes were replaced with a gradual blackness.

CHAPTER 22

DANTE

DANTE SHOOK HIS HEAD REPEATEDLY, trying to clear up his vision and recover from what he'd just experienced. For the last several minutes, he'd seen everything that happened through Conner's eyes, and he actually felt a mixture of relief and sorrow at the return to his own reality.

"Son, this program was designed to spare you from the most painful parts of my experience. Once we were separated and taken to different parts of the ship, the aliens ceased their gentle behavior and began behaving . . . well, they began behaving like we would, were we to bring home an extraterrestrial. Greta and I never spoke about what happened to us, and until now, I only shared with John and the others the most necessary parts, leaving out as many of the horrors as I could. Honestly, son, it's still too painful for me to go into exact details about what happened to me on board that ship . . . and Greta . . . poor Greta. I'll say enough so that you understand what's happening, though."

"The first thing they did was inject me with some sort of serum, which caused my muscles to expand to their greatest capacities and probably affected me in other ways, as well. After this, they performed a variety of experiments on my physical being and my pain thresholds. Then they injected me with another vial of some sort of glowing, greenish liquid. At the time, I had no idea what it was, and admittedly I was in no frame of mind to even consider the ramifications. By now, I'm sure you have found out that your DNA is slightly different from the average human's. I believe that it was this injection that caused that. We soon found, though, that the only consequences of your DNA change were all positive, in that you seemed to be stronger, faster, and smarter than any other child your age. That's why we never told you or your mother, or anyone outside of the scientists working on the case. I'm sure even John thought that I was left in the dark, but I always had my suspicions, which were eventually confirmed for me behind closed doors.

"The next . . . and last . . . thing that happened to me, though . . . it could prove disastrous. Without going into too much detail, what happened was they . . . used my sperm to impregnate one of their own females, much as they used one of their own males to impregnate Greta. The only thing that I know about the child is that it's a boy . . . probably with greater variations of the gifts you received. Although everything that had transpired thus far was horrible beyond description, what happened next warrants our worries about an invasion. Just before they sent us back to the vessel, the spacecraft passed an inhabited planet. They transported down and wiped out the planet's residents in hardly any time at all. Apparently each of these creatures has a personal forcefield that prevents any projectile weapon fire from getting past. This makes the aliens virtually unstoppable by most means of warfare. They showed their victims no mercy and, from the looks of the some of the rooms I saw in the spacecraft, this wasn't their first conquest by a long shot.

"As you can see, we took these events to mean the worst. Once I returned, during the months your mother was pregnant, John and I, with a small group of scientists, went over everything that had happened on that mission and tried to prepare for every eventuality. We came to a few simple conclusions. The alien creatures would use what they learned from myself and Greta to eventually attempt an invasion of Earth. Knowing what little we did about them and their forcefields, we came to the conclusion that only more primitive weapons could be used against them. You will find the prototype of a specially designed weapon elsewhere in this room. We don't know for sure if it will work, since we were never able to obtain any hard data about the forcefields, but it is the best we can do.

"That brings me to the hardest thing I've ever had to say to you. Right now, as I'm making this tape, you are 4 years old and already exhibiting many special talents, foremost being your lung capacity. Have you ever noticed how you never seem to lose your breath, or how you never have any problems staying underwater longer than everyone else does? When you were much younger, I ran a series of do-it-at-home tests on you, without anyone else's knowledge or consent. I found that your skin is tougher than that of a normal human, and you really don't need to breathe. I believe that the only reason you do so is because of instinct. Combined with your superior strength and mental prowess, you are our best . . . maybe our only . . . hope for survival if the aliens ever come. You are connected to them, through your DNA, and you will probably feel . . . somehow . . . when and if they make a move towards Earth.

"Regrettably, I can see that the time allotted for this private recording is growing short, and very possibly my time as well. I wish that there were some other way that this could be handled, but if we wait for an invasion there would be too much panic and unnecessary death. You must be the first line of defense . . . of offense . . . of hope. All the specific details of the plan are outlined in the papers in this very box. I wish that I could be there to help you deal with all of this, but another of the conditions of you hearing this tape was my death. I'm sorry, son . . . I'm sorry that it has to be you. I want you to know that I love you, and that I'm always with you . . . no matter what. Please . . . be careful . . ."

The tape recorder finally ran out of tape and shut off. Dante had tears in his eyes and even more questions on his mind, but now he finally knew that everything was up to him. He knew that he would do his best to succeed, not only for the sake of the planet, but for his father as well.

INTERLUDE

"It seems like the father left behind more than I anticipated," Ulysses said. "Perhaps it's time I gave our friend a little bit more to deal with . . . and let him know just how conflicted he should really be when the time comes to choose."

Ulysses smirked, watching all of the creatures that inhabited the ship along with him continue about their work, pretending not to hear him. Through years of nearly constant torture and violence, he'd trained them to let nothing stand in the way of the job set before them. Occasionally, there would be an exception, a creature mistakenly believing he could free his kin or perhaps even take control of everyone for himself, but such rebellions were always squelched immediately and with finality. In this instance, he felt a strong desire to see the creatures lose hope, to feel their fear. Reaching out with barely any effort, he grabbed the closest one, squeezing the black, scaly arm nearly to the point of dislocation.

"What do you suggest we do to display to Dante the great seriousness of the situation?"

Ulysses reveled in the terror he could see in the creature's pupilless eyes at the realization that it had no true grasp on what it was being asked. With barely any effort, he flung the creature back against the wall, using only enough force to make a point, while avoiding any permanent damage. At this point in the game, it wouldn't do to lose any more members of his force. Even though his plan had been set in motion long before the latest developments with Dante and his governments "secret base," Ulysses had several potential chess pieces to move on the board. Over the years, he'd made it his top priority to learn and understand every part of Dante's life, in preparation for the day . . . and choice . . . he knew was inevitable. This was more than a simple invasion to him. It was a matter of pride and honor, and it was the final step in a lifelong journey that he always knew would draw him in this direction.

"I do believe it's time to remind Dante of who is and isn't truly a part of his family," he said, heading to the control room.

* * *

CHAPTER 23

GWEN

AFTER FINALLY REGAINING ENOUGH COMPOSURE to set aside the pregnancy test, Gwen went about the business of packing for her somewhat-forced trip to see her parents. Although Dante had always gotten along well with them, he had never once requested a trip to see them, so just by bringing them up specifically, she knew something serious was going to happen. In all the years she'd known John, the one thing she hated about him was that he never seemed to be completely honest with anyone. She understood that part of it was his job and the fact that he simply couldn't tell anyone every detail, or in some cases any detail, of whatever was happening in his life at the time. She trusted him, and time and again he'd come through for her whenever she needed someone. Gwen would always be grateful to him for introducing her to Dante, but now, here he was taking him away from her when she needed him most.

Shaking off the clinginess she was beginning to feel as a side effect of the pregnancy, even though she understood it was more about the danger she felt Dante was heading into, she absentmindedly placed her clothes into a suitcase. Even though she felt she could take care of herself, she now had another potential life to think about, and that was going to have to take precedence over her desire to stay home and wait by the phone. As she was moving clothes around, she accidentally knocked over a box containing relics from her past. Gwen looked closely at her Bachelor's Degree in Secondary Education, wondering exactly what she was thinking when she chose that for a career path. While she loved all the kids, sometimes she felt as if there were someone better suited to the job, someone with a less dramatic life.

Shaking that thought from her already too-cluttered mind, she once again looked at her cell phone, wondering if Dante had made it to the airport safely. She considered calling her parents, but then thought better of it, as she had no intention of rushing to get there. As she sat there thinking, she decided it would be nice to look in on Dante's mom, Becky, before heading off to Tampa. If she could build up the courage to tell Becky about her impending grandchild, then she knew they'd be able to spend some time celebrating the news. *Anything to take my mind off of everything else.* Taking a final look around to see if she was forgetting anything, Gwen headed down to her car, hoping that the next time she returned home, her family would be whole once again.

CHAPTER 24

BECKY

Moving to Miami hadn't been part of Becky Smith's plan, but neither had losing the man she loved at such a young age for poor Dante. She felt she'd done the best she could under the circumstances that life had given her, but there were days that she could do nothing but remember the past. Sometimes the memories would come expectedly when she would look through old picture albums or talk to Dante on the phone, but there were other times, more and more lately it seemed, that even something as simple as washing the dishes could trigger intense memories of the past . . . or her life with Conner, before the accident. *Very good, Becky. You say accident almost as if you truly believe that's what it was.* The sound of a ringing phone pulled her out of the daze she was suddenly feeling, but enough fog was left in her mind that she nearly tripped over her own two feet in the rush to answer it.

"Hello, Smith residence, Becky speaking . . . unless you're selling something. In that case, this is a very clever answering machine message my son taught me how to record . . ."

For a moment, laughter was the only thing Becky heard on the other end of the phone, but it was a joyful laughter that she immediately recognized.

"Oh, Gwenny! How are you? Are you kids coming to visit? I've been cleaning all day, but there's still so much to do . . ."

"Oh, hush, mom . . . your house is never anything other than spotless and you know it," Gwen's voice had a slight, noticeable tint of nervousness. "No, Dante's . . . away on business, but I thought I'd swing by and see if you wanted to go with me to visit my parents for a few days. It's been ages since they've seen you, and they were . . ."

Becky cut her off mid-sentence, "Sweetie, I'm the widow of a military man and the mother of a very gifted special agent. If I can tell when both of them are feeding me bologna, I can sure tell when you're not giving me the whole story. Spill it, dear."

Silence was the only reply, carrying on to the point that Becky felt the need to check if her connection was still good.

"I'm sorry . . . I don't know everything, "Gwen sobbed her reply. "I'm on my way to your house, I'll explain everything then. Don't worry, Dante's fine . . . he's just . . . John came, and . . ."

Becky sighed and shook her head, feeling a heaviness set upon her that she hadn't felt since Dante had retired from the FBI. If Dante was taking another mission, much less if John was involved again, then she knew everything was much more serious than Gwen was even letting on at the moment.

"Just come in when you get here, Gwen . . . I've just been hit with the worst headache, and I'm going to rest my eyes for a few moments," Becky said, as images and memories flashed uncontrollably through her mind.

Not giving Gwen a chance to worry over the phone, Becky clicked the end button and slowly, feebly lowered herself to the ground, leaning up against the kitchen cabinets. It seemed as if her life was flashing before her eyes, in agonizing detail. She could plainly see herself as a young child, being raised by her two loving parents that tried desperately to give her everything they'd never had growing up in the Depression. Although they never had much to spare, Becky knew they always had just enough money to get by from meal to meal, from day to day, and for that she had always been grateful. As that memory dissolved into the next, she wondered why she was being given the gift, and in some ways curse, of seeing her life spread out before her in her mind's eye.

Before the next series of images flashed, a strange shortness of breath took her by surprise and brought with it a sense of panic and urgency, and if not for the fact her heart and the left side of her body felt fine, she would swear she was having a heart attack or a stroke. Becky reached for the counter top, trying to pull herself to her feet, but her hand slipped and she toppled the rest of the way to the floor. For just a moment, everything cleared up, except for one memory . . . the last day she ever spent with Conner.

INTERLUDE

"Get up, sweetheart, you've got to see what Dante's doing now! It's amazing," the enthusiasm in Conner's voice more than made up for the early hour of the day.

Becky slowly opened her eyes, smiling immediately at the slightly wrinkled but still dashing face of her husband of fifteen years. She loved the joy he radiated whenever he talked about his four year old son, a miracle they'd both been thrilled to receive after ten years of marriage. His work, as well as life's problems, had always seemed to get in the way of starting the family they both wanted.

"What is it this time, dear?" She asked, knowing that anything and everything Dante did was impressive to his father, something else she loved about him.

"He's reading, quick . . . you've got to come and see!" Conner gently pulled Becky out of bed and led her to Dante's room, where he sat on his little Spider-Man chair reading out loud to his stuffed animals.

"Yes, I've seen him read before, Conner, what's . . ." Becky stopped mid-sentence and turned her attention back to their son, trying to hear exactly what he was reading. "Is that . . . is he reading *The Odyssey*?"

"The English prose translation, but still . . . for a four year old, that's quite impressive, wouldn't you say?"

Becky had no initial response. Although Dante was her first child, she was fairly sure there weren't many four year olds able to read something that challenging, and in fact, she would have been nearly as impressed with him reading a bedtime story on his own.

"It's . . . he really is your son, Conner," Becky said, filled with a sense of pride, but also a nagging feeling of worry. "Should we tell John?"

Becky nearly flinched as the joy in Conner's face was quickly replaced with a much harder, rougher look at the mention of John's name. Although he had barely said two sentences about his final mission for NASA a few years ago, John's visits had been nearly non-existent since Conner's return.

"No, no, this is just for us," Conner said, obviously trying to mask his anger at John. "As long as I'm around, we will raise Dante as just a normal little boy . . . maybe a gifted normal little boy . . . but he's ours."

Becky was a little confused at Conner's response, but she didn't want to ruin the moment for any of them, so she simply nodded and hugged him, then rushed into Dante's room to pick him up. Nearly lost amidst the giggles of her little boy, Gwen barely noticed Conner reach for the hall phone that hadn't had a chance to ring more than once. She kept most of her attention on her son, but out of the corner of her eye, she saw Conner's shoulders slump, as he silently conversed with whoever was on the other end.

"Guys, I need to . . . there's something I have to take care of right now," Conner said, coming in to gently hug his family. "I'll . . . do my best to get back soon."

"Conner, what's wrong? Who was that?" Becky asked.

"It was John. There's something I'm needed for at the base," Conner replied, his hug growing stronger.

"You're needed here. They had you for too much of your life, and now it's our turn," Becky said, feeling a mix of fear and anger. "Please, let John take care of whatever it is by himself this time."

Although she was unsure why, Becky felt a terrible sense of dread at the thought of Conner going back to the base. She only knew bits and pieces of what happened there, only what Conner felt was safe to tell her, but she knew enough to know that everything there was a matter of life and death to everyone involved, sometimes literally.

"I'm only going to tell John in person to lose my number," Conner said, sliding his hand across Dante's messy, black hair. "He'd never listen over the phone, but I think in person I can convince him. I'm retired, and I'm sure there are better people than me he can rely on now."

"There are no better people than you, but please, let's just invite him over to the house tonight for dinner. You'll see, he'll come, and he'll meet Dante, and everything will be fine. You'll be able to stay home. Call him back, Conner, please," Becky felt guilty at the surge of emotions she was feeling to convince Conner to stay, but she didn't question it.

"He won't listen. I tried, Beck. Whatever it is, I think it has something to do with what happened . . . with Greta . . . and the last mission."

Becky knew better than to question the details of the last mission, as she'd done a few times over the year. She knew Conner would share with her all that he could, but she also could tell how painful the memory was for him, and forcing him to relieve that pain had never been worth it . . . until now.

"What happened, Conner? What does John have over you?"

There was a long pause, as Conner stood completely still, staring off into the distance at nothing in particular.

"I have to go this time. John knows . . . he wouldn't call unless I had to be there," Conner said. "I promise, I'll tell you everything when I come home. Everything."

"I don't care about that. Just come home," Becky hugged him tightly and kissed his cheek, then held Dante up to do the same.

Conner smiled and kissed her lightly on the forehead, then did the same to Dante. She could see a new glistening in his eyes, as if he were holding back tears, and it scared her more than anything else ever had. Still, their departure was silent, and her only lasting memory of her husband was a loving, apologetic stare as he looked back at her and Dante, then walked out of the house for the last time.

CHAPTER 25

BECKY

"Conner . . ."

Becky slowly regained consciousness, not even remembering fully blacking out, and tried once again to regain her footing. Everything hurt, though, and the weakness that had hit her during the memories wasn't going anywhere. She prayed that Gwen would forget about her and go on to her parents' house, but more than that, she prayed for Dante's safety. Although Dante hadn't shown as public an interest in religion as she or Conner had hoped, she knew he still at least respected her beliefs. *Oh, Dante . . . I love you so much . . . your father would be so proud.* Although they didn't see each other as much as she'd like, Becky was one of the lucky ones, knowing how much her son and daughter-in-law loved her. Even with the early loss of Conner, she felt like her life had seen more than its fair share of love and happiness. Sometimes she had to work to see it in certain situations, but she had no regrets. Even in the darkest of times, immediately following Conner's death, trying to raise a gifted four year old boy on her own, her faith never left her.

Dimly, she was aware of a car door slamming outside, and for a moment, a sense of hope filled her, and she began to regain her strength and composure. She tried in vain to call out for Gwen, but her voice had left her along with her sense of balance. Bracing herself, she worked on standing up again, and this time had some success, managing to get up to one knee.

"Gwen, hurry, I fell . . ." she whispered, hardly able to even hear herself.

As she heard the key in the door, another memory rocked her so violently that she fell to the floor with enough force to knock the breath out of her. This time, though, she realized, it wasn't a memory, or even something from her life. She couldn't quite grasp what it meant, and she could feel herself slipping back into unconsciousness. She'd been around long enough to recognize the signs of what these feelings of weakness and shooting pain through her head probably meant at her age, even though she'd always been in good health. She tried to focus on an image of Conner and Dante, hovering over her, loving her, but it was suddenly and violently ripped away, and replaced with something else, something she didn't recognize. She felt afraid, even more afraid than the day Conner had left the house, and she felt a presence in her mind. Something screaming at her, berating her and her family. *Calling me mother?* The last thing she heard was a knock at the door, followed by a scream, and then she lost herself in the light.

CHAPTER 26

GWEN

For the rest of her life, Gwen would be unable to get two things out of her head from the day she ran into Becky's kitchen to find her motionless on the kitchen floor. The first was the obvious shock of seeing a woman she loved very much, her mother-in-law, sprawled out across the kitchen floor with her eyes wide open, holding her with a terrified stare. The second was the echo of maniacal laughter coming from everywhere and nowhere all at the same time. She had no idea how she'd ever explain either thing to Dante, especially since she had no idea when she'd even see Dante again. Even though she was fairly sure Becky was already gone, she called 9-1-1 and raced to her side anyway.

"Mom, please . . . wake up . . ." Gwen pleaded while gently shaking Becky's crumpled body.

She had no idea how much time passed before the paramedics arrived and pulled her away from Becky. The tears that filled her eyes felt selfish, as they were almost more for her need for Dante to be there than for the loss of such a wonderful woman and influence in her life. From the first time Dante took her home to meet his mom, Gwen felt a strong connection with Becky. Both women shared a strong sense of independence and the ability to lighten the mood of even the most serious room, sometimes just by their presence. Gwen's own relationship with her parents had always been decent, but she'd never really understood how close a family could be until she'd met Becky. Her faith and her love shone through in everything she did, and she had managed to raise Dante into an amazing man on her own. Just the thought of losing her husband sent chills down Gwen's spine, and it reminded her how much she admired Becky for her seemingly endless supply of strength. Gwen felt sorely in need of some of that strength, as the weight of losing the woman that had been like a mother to her in addition to not knowing what was going on with her husband and the normal worries that go along with a first pregnancy began to take their toll on her.

"Ma'am, I'm truly sorry for your loss," one of the paramedics said.

Gwen absentmindedly nodded and attempted to answer all of the questions they asked her, as they loaded Becky's body into the back of the ambulance. She knew they were just doing their job, but part of her resented them for it. She resented herself for not getting there sooner, and she even resented John for pulling away her husband at the most crucial time in her life. *My baby . . . Dante, where are you?* After several minutes of questioning, which she vaguely understood was as much to get Becky's information as to test Gwen for shock, the paramedics left her everything she'd need to give to the funeral home and claim the body, once Dante was home . . . if Dante came home. Once they were finally gone, Gwen sat in the front seat of her car, with the radio on full blast and the air hitting her in the face and drying her tears, and did something she hadn't done since marrying Dante. She prayed.

CHAPTER 27

DANTE

DANTE HAD NO IDEA HOW long he stood, silently staring at the tape recorder his father had left for him. A strange feeling of loss flowed through him, causing him to shudder, and wonder yet again what exactly was going on with him.

"Dante . . . I know it's quite a shock for you to find out all of this, but . . ."

Dante turned around and grabbed John by the collar before he had a chance to finish his thought. Being separated from his wife and home, being dragged back into the midst of something that had apparently been on John's radar for Dante's whole life, he felt a flush of anger rushing over him. All the unanswered questions and all the manipulations he'd put up with from John over the years had built on top of each other, and now that wall was crashing down.

"You know. YOU know. How long have you known this? Did you know it that day my senior year when we met? Did you know it when you introduced me to Gwen? Did you know it when dad died?"

John tried futilely to loosen Dante's grip, "Son, you're hurting, Conner's death was a shock for all of us. If you need someone to blame, I'm more than willing to take it, but you've got to try to calm yourself . . . more than just your feelings are at stake here."

Dante shoved John back a few feet, part of him wishing that guards would burst in and allow him to burn off some of his anger. Still, he knew John was right in at least one thing, this wasn't about Dante's feelings, but he was tired of getting the runaround from John on everything, and it was past time to get all the answers. Taking a moment to gather himself, Dante's mind raced through the events of the last few weeks, in particular everything he'd learned since the sun came up yesterday. He'd always been good at logically and analytically looking at everything there was to learn from any given situation. Many considered this "gift" to be over thinking, and in some ways, they'd be right. As a member of the CIA, though, this obsession with detail was quite useful. Dante knew that Gwen had called John on the day she took him to the hospital, but it hadn't dawned on him that John had shown up faster than a normal "friend" probably would be able to shut down things, much less someone still entrenched in CIA work. Following this thought process through, Dante realized that his visions had been slightly more informative and less painful since John arrived. It was entirely possible this was a coincidence, but, with everything in his life hanging in the balance, he wasn't about to give John the benefit of any doubt anymore.

"Twice now you've known a little too much about my visions, and when they begin and end . . . and I get the feeling it's got nothing to do with anything physical I'm doing to give them away. Wait . . . how did dad know on the tape recorder I would have one about his experience? What triggered that?" Dante took a step towards John, keeping his gaze directly into John's eyes, letting him see firsthand the anger Dante was feeling. "My life's been ripped apart, and I'm starting to wonder just how much you've had to do with it over the years."

Dante stepped in between John and the exit, completely forgetting about the files and papers left behind by his father for the moment.

"Son . . ."

"Let's go back to just 'Dante' until I hear your answer."

"Dante, it's not like that. Your father . . . when he died, he told me to take care of you, to bring you along, to get you ready for this. He knew what might happen. He was a very brave man," John said.

Dante paused, as something clicked in him that never had before, though now he wondered why he'd never once thought about it in depth. He'd long accepted the fact that his father's death wasn't everything it appeared to be, but until now, in this base, he'd never really felt the need to question exactly what happened that day.

"How did he really die? It wasn't an accident on the way to the lab that day, was it?"

John cleared his throat, obviously attempting to regain his composure, "Dante, we can discuss this later. You have to . . ."

"I don't have to do anything until I get answers," Dante said.

Before John could reply, the room went dark for a split second, and when the lights returned, Dante could feel a vision coming, but it felt off, slightly different than usual. It was more painful than before, but it wasn't as jumbled and puzzling as most of them had been in the past. This time it seemed to be a direct view into some moment in the past, rather than a possible glance into the future.

"John . . ." Dante gasped as he collapsed to the floor in agony.

INTERLUDE

"John, I'm done with all of this. I don't care what you found or what flowery speech you're planning on giving, but I'm out. I'm going to go home and raise my family, and that's that."

"Conner, you could have told me that over the phone," John said, trying and failing to lighten the mood. "I want nothing more than to let you go home to Becky and Dante, but this was too big not to bring you in on it, and unfortunately, it's probably going to have an effect on Dante, as well."

Conner sighed and sat down at the table, glancing at the tape recorder and files scattered all over. Although they were definitely not typical reading, all of the facts and figures about aliens, specifically the creature that killed Greta from the inside out, were things that had already been brought to his attention. In fact, they were things he desperately wished he could forget, though often he'd wake up in the middle of the night in a cold sweat, momentarily feeling like he was still back on the spaceship.

"I know all this, John. Let's cut through all the games and manipulations, and please just tell me why I'm here," Conner said, quickly losing what little patience he had.

John nodded and motioned for him to follow, "This way . . . and bring the tape recorder."

Although he didn't understand why John would make such a request, Conner grabbed the tape recorder and followed, playing along at least for the moment. Despite everything, John had always played as straight with him as possible, sharing occasional classified information at times that Conner really started to question things. Conner knew that even sharing a little information was a subtle manipulation by John, to earn his trust, but he also knew that his intentions were honorable. Recognizing the room they were entering, Conner began to feel the sense of dread from before grow quite a bit stronger.

"We're going to see 'it,' aren't we?"

Conner shuddered as John sullenly nodded his head, then turned and entered a special unlock code for the most secure and secret section of the base. Conner lowered his head upon walking in, but even that wasn't enough to keep him from catching a glimpse of the deceased black, scaly creature lying on a cold slab of metal in the center of the room. Even though he knew it was only partially related to the race of creatures that had tortured and experimented on him, the simple fact that it bared such a resemblance to them was enough to bring all the bile in him to the forefront. *I hate you . . . for what you did to Greta, for what your kind has done to me.* Over the years, he'd managed to direct all his hate and pain from that mission onto this creature, even though he knew it had less than nothing to do with what had occurred.

"I know this is the last place you want to be, so I'll make this as brief as possible," John motioned for the four guards and two scientists to leave the room. "As you know, this is the creature that Major Williams . . . brought back with her from your final mission."

"I thought you'd locked it in the morgue after you finished the autopsy," Conner still couldn't bring himself to look directly at it. "What could possibly have caused you to bring it back out now?"

John cleared his throat, "We didn't. Four hours ago, the alarm sounded and when we got here to check it out, it was here, as you see now. Conner, our response time was under 30 seconds, and nothing appeared on any of the cameras. Simply put, we have no idea what happened."

For the first time, Conner raised his gaze to meet the creature's pupilless eyes, allowing himself to remember the first time he'd seen such soulless, dead eyes nearly five years ago in a sector of space that still remained uncharted. Conner wondered if somehow the creature was still alive, and was simply faking it right now to lure him in closer. After all, they still knew next to nothing about how the creatures lived and died, since this "thing" had been stillborn. Conner stifled the urge to take a step back, and instead moved forward, joining John near the creature's head.

"I agree that's something that should be investigated, but even when I was a part of this, that wasn't my expertise. So I ask again, John, why am I here?"

John handed Conner a small, clear evidence packet, containing a sliver of metal that appeared to be inscribed with something. Conner held it close and immediately recognized the metal as being from the spaceship that had captured him, or at least the same type of metal.

"Πατέρα, ο θάνατος του γιου σας θα σηματοδοτήσει το τέλος της Οδύσσειας," Conner read the inscription shakily. "Greek. 'Father, your son's death will mark the end of the odyssey.' Where did you get this?"

"It was in the creature's mouth when we got here," John said. "Conner, we'd been through every inch of this thing and nothing like this had ever been discovered. I hate to say this, but it has to be a sign or a warning from . . . well, from them."

Thinking through what he'd just learned, Conner's mind flashed to the image of the family he'd left at home. His wife, Becky, standing there watching him leave, and his son heading back to the book he'd been reading before their family moment had interrupted him. *The Odyssey.* Conner had seen enough over the years to know that it couldn't be a coincidence, but at the same time, it made no sense. Even if the creatures he'd encountered had a way to track him, they'd never had contact with Dante in any way. It was then that he wondered how much John actually knew about them, and just how much they were able to affect his reality, as they'd done with the creature's body in this room.

"John, I understand the gravity of this situation, but . . . why me? Surely you have more capable minds employed here to help you figure out what this means."

"Turn it over, Conner."

Conner flipped the evidence packet over and inspected the back of the metal sliver. His heart began racing, and he had to lean on John for support as he read what was inscribed. *Conner.* He felt as if the room was crashing in on him, and the only logical part left active in his mind told him that someone had to be playing a joke on him. Even after making the connection with "odyssey," Conner still had clung to the notion that not everything could be so neatly tied together. There was no doubt he recognized the metal, and, to his knowledge, no one at the base would have anything to gain from engraving his name on a cryptic Greek quote.

"I wish more than anything that I had answers for you this time," John said. "Every time we've tried to test this metal, our equipment has malfunctioned. All we know is that roughly four hours ago, something or someone was here and then wasn't. You've got to believe me . . . this time I'm not being vague to protect the nation's interests, or even my own. I just don't know."

Conner dropped the equipment packet and the tape recorder to the ground and stared at the creature lying so still and peaceful on the metal slab. Moving faster than he had in years, Conner flipped the table across the room, sending the deceased creature flailing to the ground and snapping its neck. Without even looking in John's direction, he turned and left the room, heading back to the top secret files containing all the information they had on this creature and its race. For a moment, he considered ripping them to shreds and leaving the base behind forever, going home to just hold his wife and son until he couldn't hold them any longer. Even in this state, though, part of him knew that he had to act in the best interests of Dante's future. Even if this was some insane trick by the government, he had to play along to insure his son's safety. Part of him wanted to run back to Becky and Dante, take them in his arms, and then run away somewhere with them, somewhere no one would ever find them. Another part wanted to follow whatever John's instructions were going to be and see this through to the end, so that hopefully his son would never have to be sitting where he was today.

"We're working from way behind here, so I'll wrap this up for you," John said, placing the tape recorder before him. "We need you to record a message for Dante, just in case we don't make it through this. He's obviously going to be a central figure in whatever is going to happen, and, regardless of how much you think you've hidden from me, I know he's got special gifts because of whatever happened to you on that spaceship."

"What do you want me to say?"

Conner felt all the desire to fight circumstances leave him for a moment, as a feeling of despair and loss crept over him. He remembered that final mission with Greta like it was yesterday. The events had always been burned into his brain, and he'd always had a desire to share them with Becky in order to let them go and attempt to move on without seeing them whenever his eyes would shut. However, he still was an old fashioned man, and he knew that even knowing what she knew, she would always wonder if there was more she could do to help him. Conner wished he'd never entered the air force, never worked his way into NASA, and, above all, never met the man that was currently asking him for one more mission. He didn't truly resent John, but he saw him as the living embodiment of everything that had been taken from him and everything that was about to happen to him and his family.

"We'll figure that out in due time. Do you remember anything at all about the creatures . . . about that mission? Anything you haven't shared yet?"

Conner thought back, "They all had metal bands on one wrist. Some type of personal force field. I could feel resistance when I tried to hit them, and I saw one activated out of the corner of my eye in some kind of training exercise. They're not necessarily violent, just . . . scientifically curious, I think."

Conner had no idea why all of this popped in his head at that moment. In fact, he hadn't ever intended on keeping it from his colleagues, especially since it had little to do with the events that had taken place and permanently changed his and Gwen's lives. Nothing about this situation felt like it made any sense to him, and he wasn't at all sure how or why any extraterrestrial creatures would have any interest in him or his family. Even if the aliens had altered his DNA and intended him to have a child, the government had poked and prodded him to the point that there was no chance that the creatures had planted any kind of a tracking device on him.

"Considering all you've gone through, I'm going to find a way to sneak that information into a 'lost' file that I just happened to 'find,'" John said, looking absently at the evidence packet in his hand. "Conner, I have an idea. Come with me."

Conner followed John through a series of doors, each seeming to be more and more secure, all the while carrying that infernal tape recorder with him. For the next few hours, Conner did everything that was asked of him, with no thought to anything except for the safety of his wife and child that depended on him to come home. Even knowing that everything he was doing was potentially for the safety of everyone on earth, there had never been a time where Conner had wished harder that he'd just listened to Becky and stayed home.

CHAPTER 28

JOHN

"Let me go," Dante said, clearly shaking off the effects of the last vision.

John waved off the medical personnel that had crowded around him, trying to gauge his vital signs and having little success and understanding the data they were receiving. As of now, he was the only person in the room with a full grasp on Dante's unique circumstances. By the end of the day, he was sure that would change, as the "need to know" basis the information was on would stretch to everyone in the base, but for now, he wanted to keep Dante as calm as possible. Obviously, having a group of curious scientists and military personnel following him and staring at his every move would have the opposite effect on him. John had always dreaded the day he'd have to tell Dante everything, and part of him had always wished his time would be past before it came, so that a computer or disc could do the job for him. Everything about their friendship would change after this, and John had prepared himself to let go of it through a lifetime of holding on to as few attachments as possible.

"What did you see?" John asked.

"This room. 30 years ago. You and dad, the engraved metal . . . and I'm guessing the last day of his life."

John took great pride in his ability to read and understand people and situations, and just as he knew all those years ago with Conner, he knew now was a time in his life he would have to be straight forward. It wasn't a feeling he completely enjoyed, not because he liked manipulating people, but because he always worried that with too much information, anyone could become a threat or, worse yet, put their own lives in jeopardy. Most people that knew him blamed his secretive and manipulative personality on a lifetime of CIA work, but the truth was his personality was what had drawn the CIA to him in the first place. Even as a child, he'd learned the value of keeping certain details to himself and only sharing what benefited any given situation. Most of the time, he was content to use his "gifts" on his parents and any teachers that had an issue with him, but over time, he'd found it was much easier to manipulate people than to befriend and care about them. He realized how shallow and empty that sounded, but, always a master at justifying, he simply had always told himself it was for the best of everyone else.

"It was. As you'll see soon, we spent several hours preparing things for you, just in case we got to this point and either Conner or myself weren't around to guide you," John said calmly. "At the end of the recording you just heard, Conner screamed something about the spaceship and passed out. He never regained consciousness."

"So you thought the best course of action was to fake a car crash," Dante said. "That's something we'll discuss later in depth. Count on that, John."

Even after all the preparation he'd done for this moment, Dante's words still cut through John's defenses and left a pain he'd not felt since his father's death. His one mostly honest connection had always been his niece, Gwendolyn, but part of him always felt a similar connection to Dante. Granted much of that was over the guilt he sometimes let himself feel for Conner's death and the circumstances surrounding it, but he saw so much of Conner in Dante that he always allowed himself to believe that there was a sliver of hope he'd understand all that John had done. John wasn't an avid fiction reader, but he knew that every story had its heroes and its villains. After spending a lifetime convincing himself he was a hero, John saw the truth of the definition of hero standing before him in Conner's son. Perhaps there was still a place for him in the role of sacrificing hero, willing to do whatever it takes to save the world, but there were times, this being one of them, that John felt he tended more towards the villain role. Not for the evil or chaos that most villains caused, but for the sense of self preservation and manipulation that nearly all masterminds showcased during the hero's greatest moments.

"Understood," John sighed. "For now, though, I believe you have some files to look through."

John led Dante back to the area of the room with the recorder and the files. A sense of déjà vu reminded him that he'd been in a nearly identical circumstance in the exact same place 30 years ago with Conner, but he made a silent promise to himself that this time would turn out differently. Over the years, he'd learned more about the visions and their cause, as well as everything humanly possible to know about Dante's DNA, and he hoped that all of that, combined with Dante's own heroic tendencies, would be enough to sway circumstances to a much more pleasing result. Today had been a day of painful questions and answers, and John knew that the more that came out, the more answers he'd have to give. For now, though, the only thing that mattered was preparation . . . a thought that both comforted and terrified him.

CHAPTER 29

GWEN

GWEN HAD EVERY INTENTION OF following through on Dante's request to stay with her parents, but after what she'd witnessed with Becky, she wasn't sure when she would get around to it. Driving aimlessly, she noticed an old Catholic church, and, even though she wasn't Catholic, her mind flashed on the idea of a confession booth. *I need to talk to someone . . . someone that can't think I'm crazy.* She whirled her car around in an illegal U-turn and slammed her brakes directly in front of the entrance. It was late enough in the day that hardly anyone was out, so she didn't have to worry about being towed, as long as she was fairly quick about her business. Upon that thought, Gwen stopped everything she was doing and wondered what exactly her business was and why she felt the need to enter a church she'd never before even noticed. She believed that there was more to life than what could be seen, but she had never fully given in to the belief in a Creator or some being that watched over everything. Still, the idea that she could find answers, especially in a time where there were so many questions, reached out to her. She felt a slight headache coming on, and for some reason, the idea of walking inside a church, baring her soul to a stranger that would listen and not judge, called out to her as the only current cure.

Walking into the church, she looked all around, trying to find the confession booth with no experience other than that from TV shows and movies. Just as she was about to give up and leave, she saw an elderly priest look at his watch and head into a small area with two doors. Following his lead, she entered the other door and sat down, not sure if she was pleased or upset that she'd been correct in her assumption. On the television shows she'd watched, people would always open up with something about being a sinner or not having been to a confession in a long time, but she couldn't quite remember the exact phrasing, so she decided the best course of action was simply being herself.

"I've got to be up front with you, Father. I'm not Catholic. I AM a Christian . . . kind of, I guess, but I've never been to a Catholic church before," Gwen said.

"Your honesty is appreciated," the priest said, coughing to cover up a slight chuckle. "It's rare, but you're not the first non-Catholic to come in seeking solace. I'm not here to convert you, just to listen, if you choose to continue. If I may ask, though, why have you come here now, miss . . . ?"

"Gwen, and I don't know. Well, I know, but it's difficult to explain," Gwen sighed. "Everything is just wrong right now, Father. And I just found out I'm pregnant . . . that's not wrong, but right now I just don't know how to handle everything."

"Let's start with the pregnancy and work our way up to 'everything being wrong.' Does the father know?"

"No, he doesn't. I'm married, don't worry . . . . and we're still together. He just . . . business called out of the blue, and I didn't think it was the right time to let him know," Gwen said. "I know he will be happy, but I didn't want to risk him being distracted thinking about me any more than he already would."

Gwen felt a strong sense of guilt causing her to wonder if she'd really kept the news from Dante to protect him or to protect herself, in case he never came back.

"It's been my experience that all relationships benefit from direct communication and honesty. At the risk of sounding like a clichéd old priest, my advice on that is to trust him and trust your relationship. Call him. You'll be glad you did, and I'm sure he will be, too. Whether or not you believe, there is Someone with a greater plan and understanding of our lives than either you or I could ever hope to have," the priest replied.

"Maybe you're right, but, well, there's something else," Gwen broke down, unable to control her crying any longer. "I'm sorry, Father, I'll be fine, please stay there. I just . . . my mother-in-law just . . . I went to visit her, and she was on the floor of her kitchen . . . alone . . . and so cold . . ."

"I am so sorry, Gwen. I can only imagine what that must have been like for you. Death is always difficult to deal with, especially during such a trying time in your life without your husband there to support you. I truly feel even stronger that you don't try to handle all of this alone, though. Is there any way you can contact your husband or even go to where he is?"

Gwen looked over at the priest through the gated window between them and blinked several times, unable to speak for the moment. She knew all of John's contact information, and if she knew they were in New Mexico at a military base, so it would be conceivable that she could find someone in the military somewhere in New Mexico that could direct her to him. Obviously she probably wouldn't be ushered onto the base, but once they knew she was pregnant or what had happened with Dante's mom, she was confident she'd be able to at least meet up with Dante somewhere. The plan sounded insane, even to her, so she decided not to share it with the priest, but she did feel a sense of peace upon reaching the decision, flawed as it may be.

"Thank you, Father. Thank you so much. This really helped," Gwen said, leaving the confessional before the priest had a chance to reply.

Racing out to her car, she tried to dial each number she had for John and Dante, always receiving a voice mail or busy signal, which she expected but had to try anyway. In the back of her mind, she wondered if she should call her parents, but she assumed Dante hadn't gone so far as to set up her visit, especially since it was a last minute decision. She feared that calling them to check would do nothing more than make them worry. For the first time in weeks, she felt like she was finally going in the right direction as she sped towards the airport. Maybe heading to New Mexico without much of an idea where she was going wasn't the best plan in the world, but it was better than sitting around her parents' house doing nothing but mourning and worrying.

CHAPTER 30

DANTE

DANTE STOOD STARING AT THE same keypad his father had used 30 years before, thinking about everything he'd faced in his life and how none of it truly prepared him for this moment. Remembering the famous, and occasionally overused quote from his old Spider-Man comics, "with great power comes great responsibility," Dante wondered whether he was least prepared for the power or the responsibility that came with it. Although he'd always known he was considered to be an elite physical specimen by his peers, he'd always just attributed it to his work ethic when it came to physical fitness and his healthy diet. Standing there, where his father had once stood, Dante wondered what his physical limits were, or if he even had any. In the back of his mind, he felt a constant nagging *I didn't get to say goodbye to her* repeating over and over again, as if someone were standing next to him whispering and trying to drive him crazy. Allowing himself to think of Gwen for only a second, Dante wondered idly what she'd told her parents about his departure once she'd arrived. Fearing thoughts of Gwen would take away his resolve to continue, he shook her from his mind and began typing in the entry code his father had left especially for him. Nothing happened.

"John, are you sure this is right?"

The fact that nothing had happened hadn't really been a surprise to Dante, as part of him still believed that this was all part of one of his visions. That any minute now, he'd wake up and see Gwen sitting next to him, holding his hand and calmly waiting through whatever seizure he'd had. Aliens, secret bases, government conspiracies, everything seemed like a bad science fiction novel more than real life.

"Positive. Conner didn't make mistakes," John said calmly, never looking up from the files he was studying. "Touch the wall."

Dante sighed heavily and reached forward, placing his hand on the wall just above the keypad. At first, he wondered if John was just playing some new mind game, trying to see if he could get him to do anything he asked, but then a loud series of clicking and whirring sounds emanated from behind where he'd placed his hand.

"Dante, you need to have a look at these files. The sooner you begin studying Conner's plan, the more chance for success you have," John said. "I'm afraid there's no way around it . . . it's extremely dangerous. I truly wish there was another way . . ."

Tuning out the rest of what John had to say, Dante instead focused on everything that was now happening in front of him. Although he knew John had been here when everything had been set up, all of this was brand new to him.

"I'll look in a second. I want to see what happens now that I've been recognized by this thing." Dante stepped back as a small section of the wall pulled back and disappeared. "As for it being dangerous, if you didn't care for the last 30 years, don't pretend to start now."

After a few seconds more of the loud clicking and whirring and seemingly random movements all along the wall, two metallic arm-like shafts extended out holding a sheathed sword. Dante stared in disbelief, both at the oddness of a sword, out of all possible things, appearing before him, as well as a curiosity to see if anything else would happen. Finally, he removed the sword from the grasp of the metallic arms, and they quietly reentered the wall, followed by more clicking and whirring. Just below where the sword had come out, two small metal boxes were gently pushed forward from within the wall, each roughly the size of a little girl's music box. Gently leaning the sword against the nearby table, Dante removed each box from its perch and sat it down, making sure not to jostle them. As he went to open one, John quickly reached out and stopped him by placing his hand firmly on the lid.

"Don't. They're not to be opened here," John said, removing his hand and placing the files out towards Dante. "Read these, you'll understand."

Dante stared at John for a moment, considering one of several questions that had formed in the last few minutes, but finally chose to take the files and skip the middle man for once. Each page was written directly to Dante, and he wondered what it had been like for his father to write several top secret documents to a son he only knew until the age of four. The first page contained schematics for a device, which as far as Dante could make out, appeared to be some sort of teleportation chamber. It seemed odd to Dante that a 30 year old file would speak of a device that, to his knowledge, had yet to be invented even in today's society. Choosing to save all his questions until the end, Dante continued through the files, carefully reading everything his father and John had planned for an invasion that they'd suspected would one day happen. One box apparently contained a bomb built to deliver a massive Electromagnetic Pulse blast, which Conner had concluded would effectively knock out operating systems in all of the spacecraft within a 200 mile radius, assuming that the aliens had made no incredible advancements in the past thirty years, something Dante felt was quite a bold assumption. Still, he trusted his father's instincts and hoped that he knew what he was doing. Immediately upon reading the contents of the second box, Dante realized why John had been so adamant about the two boxes remaining closed.

"A dirty nuke? An EMP? Why keep these hidden in a secret base? Even thirty years ago, they were fairly common," Dante said, still thumbing through the files, checking for anything he may have missed.

"Not these. Everything Conner remembered about the ship, about the aliens, about his experiences . . . every bit of information we could get from the creature's autopsy . . . we used all of that to do our best to key these to their specific systems and physiology," John said. "Honestly, Dante, we have no idea if they'll even work. I wanted to make more, to test them, but Conner refused to help unless we did everything by his rules. He didn't want any of this used for any reason other than earth's defense."

"Which explains why the teleportation device was never built," Dante said.

John cleared his throat, "Actually, we've tried for years to duplicate these schematics, and I've even overseen a few tests of various teleportation projects, but, to date, none have been successful."

Dante couldn't tell if John was being purposely vague or if the plan really was as crazy as it seemed. Knowing what he knew of John, it was hard for him to believe that, even if he'd agreed to Conner's requirements, he would have simply left everything sitting in a secret base and waiting until the day they might need it.

"Let me get this straight, basically the plan is to build a teleportation device, which may or may not work, and then stand back while I lead a force through it to place two bombs, which also have been untested. Please tell me I'm wrong on that, because, I've got to tell you that sounds like a suicide mission."

Dante felt a wave of discomfort creep through him as he stared at John silently, waiting. He couldn't tell if John was concocting a new manipulation for him, or if he truly had no idea how to answer this line of questioning.

"You do have it wrong . . . there's no force," John looked away, noticeably uncomfortable. "It's just you. We can't . . . even if we had enough time to build a teleportation device powerful enough to send a legitimate fighting force, you're right, it would be a suicide mission . . . for them. We believe . . . we believe that your unique physiology will enable you to survive in whatever atmosphere is present upon their ship without the need of any kind of extra oxygen or spacesuit protection. You have to believe me, this wasn't an easy decision for either of us, Conner . . ."

"You cannot expect me to believe my father was willing to send his own son, who I might remind you was FOUR YEARS OLD WHEN YOU MURDERED HIM, to die on an improbable suicide mission."

"I will grant you it took a great deal of convincing, but in the end, he understood it was the only way," John said, still avoiding eye contact. "Our only experience with any extraterrestrial race came from whatever happened to Conner and Greta on that mission, but until that moment when the creature's body was disturbed, it had been five years since anyone had truly even thought about them. Obviously we studied the body, but we had every reason to believe if they'd planned on attacking us, it would have happened shortly after Conner and Greta returned. As horrible as their experiences were, I'm afraid it was nothing really different than what we'd have done in their place, so we simply surmised they were similar to us in other ways."

"You're kidding yourself if you expect me to believe we wouldn't have sent a fleet to another planet we knew had life on it, if we had the ability . . ."

Dante stopped midsentence, his mind racing at a thought which had been on the outskirts of it since he had arrived at the base. It had crossed his mind earlier, just before one of the visions ripped through his brain, but then with everything else going on, he'd forgotten it.

"Why has no one heard of a warping technology that was 'successfully' tested over thirty years ago?" Dante asked, fearing he knew the answer.

John closed his eyes and lowered his head, "We can't. It . . . it all stopped working after Conner arrived back. We tried everything, but even in our own galaxy . . . nothing. There's literally no explanation."

"Except that they wanted us to stay put," Dante shook his head, realizing that his father's plan truly was the only option left. "Get it started . . . the teleportation device. I'm in."

John nodded his head and somberly picked up his telephone, calmly giving orders to whoever was on the other end. Dante tried to listen, hearing things like "get every mind in the country on this now," but his attention kept fading. Pacing nervously, wondering if he should try to contact Gwen or his mother, he accidentally kicked the leaning sword, it's loud clank momentarily pulling him out of his thoughts.

Hearing that John was still making calls, Dante picked up the sword and removed it from its sheath. Turning it over in his hands, he saw that it was inscribed, "Πατέρα, ο θάνατος του γιου σας θα σηματοδοτήσει το τέλος της Οδύσσειας." He recognized it as Greek, "Father, your son's death will mark the end of the odyssey," which was the same engraving from the small shard of alien metal that his father had handled in his last vision. The sword itself was extremely well crafted and looked brand new. Dante ran his hand over the nearly four foot long sharpened blade, trying to discern what type of metal was used to make it. It seemed to be sturdier than any stainless steel sword that Dante had seen before and had an odd familiar quality that he couldn't quite place.

"It's essentially the same metal that we believe their ship was made from, at least based on what Conner said about the sliver we found in the lab 30 years ago," John said, finally off the phone. "We did everything we could to imitate it, and even made the original piece a part of the sword, as I'm sure you noticed with the engraving. Again, I wanted to do more with it, but Conner insisted we only use it once. Your 'secret weapon' he called it."

"Secret weapon? How am I supposed to defeat an alien race using a sword, even if it is specially made?" Dante pulled the sword behind his back and then brought it forward again with a powerful practice swing.

"When Conner described what he remembered of their personal force fields, it seemed likely that they were designed to mainly stop projectiles like bullets, possibly lasers, anything they would potentially face in a battle," John said. "It's our hope that, until the EMP goes off, at least, this will provide you with at least some offensive firepower. Think about it like this . . . if you wear a Kevlar vest, and I shoot you, the bullet will stop without puncturing through. However, that same vest will allow a knife to pass through. Their metal appears to be indestructible, at least by our methods, so . . . it gives you a fighting chance, Dante."

"Indestructible? Interesting," Dante re-examined the sword and then, reacting to something John said, looked up at John quizzically. "How did you get the coordinates for me to teleport to so far in advance?"

"We didn't. There's no way for us to know the coordinates of any of their ships until they appear on our satellite radar. Based on Conner's remembrance of the interior of their ships, we should be able to use our satellite imaging to safely teleport you aboard whatever ship is most in the center of their formation," John said.

"So this really is a suicide mission . . ."

"No, of . . . of course not," John said. "It's dangerous, yes. But we believe that with your unique physiology . . ."

"Stop. Drop the CIA speak. I've already said I'm in, so the least you can do is be straight up with me right now," Dante interrupted John mid-speech.

"It could be, yes. I'm sorry," John held eye contact this time. "Even if the EMP works, even if the timer of the nuke works, even if you can survive God-knows how many aliens in a hostile environment, we have no way of knowing for sure if we'll be able to bring you home. Perhaps if we'd been working on the technology all along, but Conner feared that we'd use it for domestic purposes . . . to control our world . . . so he refused to help until these safeguards were put into place."

Dante had already known why his father would have insisted everything be kept under wraps until and only if they were needed, and, after years in the CIA and knowing everything he knew about the world and all the wars fought day after day, he felt his father had made the right call. He closed his eyes and remembered everything that he had seen in his visions involving the aliens and their systematic invasions of the two planets, and who knows how many more. He thought about their leader that seemed so bloodthirsty and violent that he was capable of absolutely any atrocity. He pictured Gwen, his family, his friends, and he knew that even though his father's plan seemed to be a probable suicide mission, there was really no choice.

"I want Gwen, her parents . . . my mother, all brought here and kept safe while I'm gone," Dante said forcefully. "And I want your assurance that you will do everything in your power to give them all everything they'll ever need if I don't come back."

John looked at Dante for a few seconds before speaking, seeming to be going over his words carefully, which concerned Dante greatly.

"I'll make the necessary calls," John said.

Even though he knew John was holding something back, Dante simply nodded his head and turned away from him, letting him exit the room to make whatever called he needed to make. Right now, the only thing he cared about was making sure Gwen and his family were as safe as possible.

CHAPTER 31

GWEN

GWEN SAT SILENTLY IN THE back of the airplane, wondering how long before it was set to touch down in New Mexico. She hadn't even gotten around to thinking about how far away the base was from the Albuquerque International airport. Maybe she would just call John or Dante repeatedly until one of them picked up. It didn't really matter, as long as she was doing something, anything, to move forward, or at the very least to not be just sitting around wondering.

"Is this your first time flying? It's my first time flying. Mommy says I shouldn't be scared, because lots of people do it all the time. So I'm not scared. Are you scared?"

Gwen was shaken from her thoughts by the sound of a little girl sitting next to her. She vaguely remembered nodding hello to the girl and her mother earlier, as they all took their seats, but shortly after the flight took off, she'd completely lost herself in thought.

"Lauren! Leave her alone. I'm sorry, she's just excited . . ." the girl's mother said.

"Oh, no it's fine," Gwen said to the woman, then turned her attention to the little girl. "No, I've flown a lot before. My uncle used to even take me out on his own plane sometimes when I was your age."

Gwen smiled as the little girl's eyes grew wide with amazement, and then her blonde pigtails bounced as she shifted her attention back to her mother, looking for approval to continue the conversation. Her mother silently laughed and nodded her head, then went back to reading the in-flight magazine.

"Your uncle had his own plane? Was he rich?"

"No, but he has a very important job, so he gets to do a lot of cool things like that. Where are you and your mommy going, Lauren?"

Once again, the little girl looked to her mother, though Gwen wasn't sure if she was looking for approval to continue talking or simply didn't know the answer to her question.

"We're going to surprise daddy," the mother said, smiling at her little girl. "I'm Vanessa, and you've already met Lauren."

"It's a pleasure," Gwen said, shaking hands with Vanessa and then with Lauren. "You have a lovely little girl. I'm sure 'daddy' will be very excited when you two arrive."

The woman laughed, "It's not exactly a surprise, but it is a little bit of a last minute trip. His business trip turned out to be a little longer than expected, and he was afraid he'd miss Lauren's fifth birthday . . . so here we are."

Lauren held up five fingers and nodded her approval to what her mother had said. The two women shared a laugh and then each politely went back to doing her own thing. After a few minutes, Gwen felt a tug on her arm and turned away from staring out the window to see Lauren's bright blue eyes staring up at her, barely able to hold in whatever question she was about to ask.

"Do you have a little girl or a little boy or are you alone?" Lauren asked quietly.

Gwen smiled, both at the innocence of the question and at the way children always seem to be able to directly get through to the heart of a situation. Gwen thought back to the positive pregnancy test and wondered if she would soon have a little girl like Lauren. The suggestion that the only other option Lauren gave her was 'being alone,' nearly brought tears to Gwen's eyes, as she pictured Dante shutting the car door behind him and heading off to meet John. Part of her wondered if she really was alone now, but this wasn't the time or place to delve into that.

"I don't have any children yet, but my husband and I are hoping to start a family really soon," Gwen said.

"Oh. Where's your husband?" Lauren returned.

For a split second, Gwen looked over to Vanessa, hoping that she would save her from this questioning, not because she didn't enjoy talking with Lauren, but because she was afraid she wouldn't be able to hold it together if it continued. Vanessa, though, seemed to be engrossed in an article and had apparently felt good enough about their short conversation that she trusted Gwen not to say anything unseemly or startling to her daughter.

"He's at work, too," Gwen said, clearing her throat in an attempt to control her emotions. "I'm going to surprise him, too."

This answer seemed to satisfy Lauren, as she went back to doodling on a little notepad she'd been holding in her lap. Gwen decided to take this chance to head towards the restroom to compose herself, before Lauren could think of any new questions to ask. Once she entered the restroom, she allowed herself to cry again, trying to keep it as silent as possible so she wouldn't draw any unwanted attention. Even though she was on her way to see Dante, she had an overwhelming feeling of grief like she'd lost him. From the time she left the church until now, she'd allowed herself to believe that her "crazy" plan was the best thing she could do, but, as she stared at her reddening eyes in the mirror, she wondered how much of that had been shock over the loss of her mother-in-law on the same day Dante had been thrown back into a part of his life she'd always dreaded he'd never truly be able to leave. Gwen had always been an independent spirit, and, even after their marriage, she'd never been the type to "need" a man around all the time. There was something different about his absence, this time, though, and she feared that it didn't have as much to do with the pregnancy as she told herself. Learning about the visions, seeing John again, everything seemed to point towards a future she had no desire to face alone.

As she gently wiped her eyes and reapplied her mascara, Gwen heard the pilot request that everyone return to their seats as they were nearing Albuquerque. Gwen blinked her eyes several times, making sure everything was back to normal and headed back to her seat. The rest of the flight passed by without incident, as Lauren had fallen asleep during Gwen's bathroom visit, and only awoke when her mother gently nudged her that the plane had landed. Gwen smiled and waved goodbye at Lauren and her mother and then headed out of the plane, turning her cell phone back on and preparing to try to reach John once again. Before she had a chance to, though, she was stopped by a pair of military men near baggage claim.

"Mrs. Smith?" The older one said, as the younger looked down at a photograph in his hands. "We've been sent by Agent John Dawson to retrieve you."

Realizing that by some miracle her "plan" had apparently worked out, Gwen breathed a heavy sigh of relief.

"Is . . . is Dante with him?"

"I'm afraid we can't reveal anything more than what we've said, ma'am. I hope you understand," the older one said, showing his identification, presumably to assure Gwen he was on the up and up. "Please come with us. We already have your luggage."

Gwen nodded her approval and decided not to waste time asking any more questions. Maybe things weren't as bleak as she feared after all. She still wasn't looking forward to letting Dante know about his mother, but at least she would have that chance now.

* * *

CHAPTER 32

JOHN

JOHN NODDED SILENTLY AS HE was informed that Gwen had landed and was on her way to the base. There would be no end to the red tape he would have to cut through in the next hour before her arrival to make sure she could even enter the top level. Still, the guilt he felt over taking Dante away from the only true family he had left was enough in this instance to force him to try. As the military personnel left him in the communications room, John wondered how different his life would have been if he'd gotten married when he had the chance. Nearly 35 years ago, he'd proposed to a beautiful young astronaut, just before she'd gone on one of her first missions, which unfortunately had also turned out to be her last. No one but Greta and he had known of their relationship, partially because he'd feared it would hurt her career, and partially because he never truly allowed himself to believe he'd found someone that could put up with everything that came along with his job. John had put his career on the line to get her involved in that mission with Conner, because he trusted that if anyone could keep her safe, it was him. Part of him wished he'd told Conner about their engagement, as he'd always intended, but there had never been a good opportunity. Telling him before the mission would have affected his preparation, and telling him afterwards simply had not been an option.

"Sir, you have a call on line one," a young agent said, fearfully peaking his head through the door and interrupting his superior.

John nodded and picked up the phone, "Agent John Dawson speaking."

The voice on the other end spoke uninterrupted for thirty seconds, then held on silently while John stared ahead for another thirty.

"I understand. Thank you," John said. "See what you can do for Gwen's parents, and tell no one else what you just told me."

John hung up the phone and sat down forcefully on the seat. When they'd found Gwen so easily, he'd made the mistake of beginning to believe that everything was going to go smoothly from here on out, but receiving the information about Dante's mother, Conner's widow, brought all the anxiety from before crashing back down upon his shoulders. The fact that Becky had apparently died in similar fashion as Conner was not lost on John, and he quickly looked to the monitors to check Dante's condition. *Still training.* Dante hadn't stopped training since John left the room, and, if Dante was still the same man he'd always known, John knew he wouldn't stop until he was told Gwen had arrived. John wondered if he should tell Dante about his mother, but then decided that it would be best to let him find out after Gwen had arrived safely. He wondered if Conner had truly been right about saving everything in secret until it was actually needed. Obviously, they would have used the technology in other areas by now, but John was beginning to think that breaking a few eggs would have been worth saving the whole omelets now. For the first time in his career, John allowed himself to wonder if he'd made a mistake.

INTERLUDE

"We need a medic," John yelled, as he ran towards the landing site.

Although he hadn't been the first on the scene, he was going to be the first to reach the crew. Once he'd seen that Conner was limping and carrying Greta, he knew that something had gone horribly wrong, but he had no way of knowing what. They'd lost communication with the shuttle hours ago, and he'd actually given up hope of seeing either one of them again.

"Conner, what happened, what's wrong?" John asked, finally reaching them, a multitude of medical personnel right at his heels.

Before Conner had a chance to answer, they were swarmed by the medics and other military personnel, and John could do nothing but stand and watch as the two people he was closest to in the world were carted off to the closest base for treatment. When they'd first heard the blip of their location emerge near where it had left, John was sure it was some type of malfunction. Partially because the odds were so against them returning after being off the grid for so long, and partially because he just couldn't bring himself to believe it until he saw it for himself. Riding in silence to the base, he wondered if there had been a problem with the warping technology or if they'd simply had some type of accident on board the ship. There had been no way for him to guess what had actually happened to the two during the hours they were missing.

Trying his best to maintain their secret, John followed Greta's unconscious body towards the medical exam lab, only to be stopped at the door and told he was unnecessary personnel. For a second, he started to fight it, but his logic prevailed, and he realized that he wouldn't be of any real help to her inside, so he headed to the observation room and waited.

Conner had been the first one to regain consciousness and gain approval for John's visitation. John spent the next several minutes trying in vain to debrief his friend, who was clearly holding back many details of whatever happened. Every few questions, Conner would stop and ask about Greta, which only confirmed for John that whatever had happened to them had been worse for her. Finally, through a lot of back and forth, John was able to piece together that there had been an extraterrestrial encounter and that the two astronauts had been separated. After it became clear that he'd gotten all he was going to for now, John left Conner alone to rest and went back to the observation area to find out how Greta was doing.

"Is there any update on the condition of Greta Williams?" John asked the lone scientist currently in the observation room.

"Ms. Williams is in a coma," the scientist replied. "We don't anticipate her recovery. The birth of the creature was clearly too much for her already stressed system."

Even though he heard the whole statement and had the obvious questions, John could only stand in stunned silence at the cold deliverance of the news that Greta could die. He didn't blame the scientist, as no one knew of their relationship, but he immediately blamed himself, which was something he'd managed to avoid for most of his career. Despite the fact that he was barely able to function now, John had to keep up appearances, especially if he had any hope of continuing to rise in the ranks at the CIA.

"What do you mean by 'creature'?" John asked calmly.

The scientist looked up from his notes, seemingly excited, "Oh, it's really quite remarkable. Somehow, Ms. Williams had carried a creature of extraterrestrial origin to gestation. It was stillborn, and we're examining it now."

John stood silently, absorbing all of the new information, as the scientist pushed past him and left the room. John gazed through the window at his fiancé and wondered if he'd lost the chance to ever tell her that she had truly been the only person he'd ever loved. As he watched, considering pushing past all the personnel and rushing to her side, he heard the all-too-familiar sound of a heart monitor loudly beeping. He didn't have to look up to know what was going to happen next and, for the first and only time in his long, illustrious career, CIA Agent John Dawson quietly and sullenly left work early.

CHAPTER 33

DANTE

As John walked into the room where Dante was focusing intently on his physical training, Dante somehow felt his presence before he ever looked towards the doorway. In addition to sensing his presence, Dante also could tell several things all at once about John's recent past. He couldn't quite focus on specific thoughts, but he detected a sadness, a sense of loss, and also a small amount of regret, something that surprised Dante even more than the growing of his abilities. Ever since he'd listened to the tape left behind by his father and felt the memory of his father's mission, Dante had wondered exactly how far his abilities would end up going. It seemed that, with enough practice, he may be able to partially read minds, though he felt like it would be more like sensing emotions or even truths and lies, more than actually reading someone's thoughts.

Since John had played with his life so much over the years, Dante decided to continue with the training and just allow him to speak when he was ready to speak. It clearly wasn't something of vital importance, or John wouldn't have wasted the time coming down to this level to find him, he'd simply have sent for him. More than likely, he was coming to tell him Gwen was close, but in reality just wanting to check on the status of Dante's training regimen. The training was no more grueling than years ago when he'd first entered the CIA, but it was very different, mostly in that it required a great deal of sword work. Guns were one thing, every agent felt as comfortable with his revolver as his own partner, but Dante hadn't done much more with a sword than play fight with Nerf swords with his college buddies. Slice at a training dummy, spin and elbow back, then jab forward with his full force . . . Dante was getting somewhat tired of the repetitive nature of the training, but he had to admit it was already feeling more comfortable.

It was definitely an odd sensation for Dante, knowing that he couldn't run out of breath. Since learning that his breathing was merely something he apparently did out of copying everyone else, he'd tested his theories and held his breath for various amounts of time. He wasn't sure if it was doing anything to help him physically, but he knew the obvious implications for space travel. The idea of going into space like his father had before him, though, was not something Dante with which Dante was extremely comfortable. He understood the importance of the mission, but everything seemed so rushed and unreal to him. At times, he expected to be hit with another crippling headache and wake up at his home, only to learn that everything had just been a dream or a figment of his imagination. In some ways, that was even the more comforting scenario, as he felt much more equipped to deal with his own potential insanity than the crazy notion that the earth was possibly going to be invaded by strange alien creatures. Until a few days ago, Dante probably wouldn't have even said he believed in aliens, much less believed that they were intelligent and potentially violent.

"It seems Gwen had a similar idea to yours about joining you on the base. We picked her up at the airport in Albuquerque twenty minutes ago," John said. "We've been . . . unable to contact anyone else in your or her family as of now."

Dante stabbed the sword into the nearest training dummy and left it there, then he grabbed a towel and wiped the sweat from his brow. The care with which John chose his last few words would have been obvious to Dante even without the young man's apparent ability to read his mentor. Something had clearly happened to someone Dante loved, or else John would have said something slightly different. He knew it wasn't Gwen, at least, because that was one thing John wouldn't hide from him, not while he needed something. Dante didn't like feeling a sense of distrust whenever he looked at John. In many ways, ever since their official meeting his senior year in high school, John had been something of a father figure to Dante.

Looking back on his life and everything they'd been through, Dante had to question everything he'd ever said and done, wondering if it was all for the purpose of training him or preparing him, or even testing him. There were so many things he wanted to bring up and discuss with John right now, and he wondered if his newfound ability to detect someone's intentions would have an impact on his understanding of John. *Still. One thing at a time.*

"I guess that shouldn't surprise me," Dante said, walking towards John. "Gwen's going to do what Gwen's going to do. One of the reasons I love her. How long until she's here?"

"Assuming no delays, her transport will arrive in forty minutes. There will be quite a bit of debriefing and security measures for her to go through, before she can even begin to join you down here, though," John said, subtly avoiding eye contact.

"When she's here, I'll go up and meet her. I want to be the one to explain all of this to her. She deserves that much, at least. Is there anywhere in the upper level that's secure?" Dante said.

Dante already knew the answer, as he'd seen the blueprints of the base among his father's secret files, but he wanted to take the opportunity to see if he could detect any changes in John's thought process between telling the truth or telling a lie, or, as John would put it, a subtle manipulation.

"Of course. I'll arrange an extra security sweep right away. In the meantime, you should attempt to get some sleep. Forty minutes isn't much, but I'm afraid it's the most you're going to have available for the foreseeable future," John said, turning to leave. "I'll make sure you're notified the moment Gwen arrives."

Even without his earlier reading, Dante knew there was something wrong with John. There had never been a time in Dante's experiences where John had seemed so frigid and professional. Obviously, he was always a CIA agent before anything else, and he carried that title very seriously, but John had always been able to read people and manipulate situations, and, in this case, he just seemed to want to leave. Dante had fully expected John to come down and pretend that he was apologetic or that they were still as close as they'd always been. Dante knew that he was vital to John's plans, so he assumed that John would do everything in his power to maintain a feeling of comfort for him. For a second, Dante considered leaving it alone and continuing to ride the waves of hate and anger he felt whenever he saw the man who had once been his father's friend and his own closest ally. However, even if everything on his mission went perfectly, Dante knew there was a decent chance he wouldn't see everyone in his life again.

"John, I'm obviously not thrilled with you. I trusted you with my life every day, and you held onto all of these secrets that you knew would one day explode . . ." Dante paused to calm himself. "But that doesn't mean I don't understand why. I may not like it, and I may not approve of your methods, but I understand your motivation. When we get through this, we'll talk. You're not going to be gone from our lives for good."

"I truly hope you're right, Dante," John sighed as he continued to walk out of the room. "Get some rest. I'll be in touch when it's time."

Dante watched as John left the room and entered the appropriate codes at the nearby elevator to leave the level. If there was one thing Dante knew John was right about these last few days, it was that he needed a break, even if it was just forty minutes. Deciding against calling for a security detail to find him a workable bed, Dante simply grabbed a fresh towel and wadded it up to use as a pillow, and then dropped to the ground. For the first time in weeks, he was able to fall asleep as soon as he shut his eyes.

INTERLUDE

"CONNER AND I WERE VERY proud of you, son."

Dante blinked his eyes quickly, unsure of where he was or what was happening. Looking around, he recognized his surroundings as his old room at his parents' house, still the same way it had been kept since he'd moved out of the house all those years ago. If this was a dream, it was the most vivid he'd ever had, but it didn't seem like a vision to him, either. He was still wearing the black shirt and spider necklace from before, and everything about his body and mind felt normal. However, he obviously couldn't have teleported somewhere without knowing it, but at the same time, he'd never really been involved personally in any of his dreams or visions. This was definitely something new, and he wasn't sure who, if anyone, might be responsible.

"Mom? Where . . . are you here?"

Dante stood up and walked through the hallway and into the kitchen, where he saw his mother, Becky Smith, looking down sadly at a seemingly random spot on the floor, near the cabinets. He felt a sense of pain from her as she looked down, and he wondered what he wasn't seeing. When he stepped closer, trying to see what she could possibly be seeing, there was a quick flash and he saw a vision of her body lying crumpled in that spot, eyes wide open and staring. Before he had a chance to ask what was going on, though, she hugged him and led him to the kitchen table, with both taking a chair and sitting. There was a long silence between the two of them, not of discomfort or fear, but just the feeling of a mother and son being reunited after some time apart. He knew it had been too long since he'd gone to visit her, and he'd yet to tell her anything about his visions or what he'd learned about his father. Still, being there with her now, whether or not it was real, he felt a sense of calmness and family that he rarely felt anymore, through no one's fault but his own.

"Don't you fret about that, sweetheart," Becky said, the smile on her face brightening the room like it always did. "That's for later. Now is for you. How are you doing out there in New Mexico? Are you eating?"

Dante wasn't sure if he wanted to laugh or cry, and he still had no idea what exactly was happening to him. He wondered if he'd finally gone crazy after all. It was definitely bordering on insane, simply because of the number of times he'd questioned his own sanity the last few days. Whether or not this was real, though, Dante fully intended to treat it as such and enjoy whatever it was.

"I'm . . . I'm fine, mom. I'm sorry I haven't been to visit you much lately. Everything has been so . . ."

"I understand. Conner explained to me about the visions and everything else that's about to happen. You don't have to worry about me. I lived a wonderful life, and I was able to watch my son grow up into such a wonderful, strong man. We're so proud of you, Dante," Becky said.

There were so many things she'd just said that Dante didn't understand, he wasn't sure where to start. Even though Conner had guessed many things quite accurately, Dante knew there was no way he'd have had a conversation about visions and possible alien threats with Becky when Dante was only four. Something was nagging at him, but the more he picked at it, the more he felt the whole experience slipping away.

"How did dad explain it to you? When he . . . he never knew about the visions. I mean, I'm sure he guessed, and he apparently knew more than he let on . . . but I was only four," Dante stumbled over his own words, trying to make sense of the situation.

"We've talked recently," Becky said. "Now don't look at your mother like she's crazy! There are two things I've always been able to keep and that's my faith and my mind. You don't have to worry that I lost either one of those, no sir."

"Mom . . ." Dante felt his head clearing slightly, but it worried him that once it did, he'd lose this moment. "How?"

"You always did know the right questions to ask," Becky laughed. "You're asleep, sweetheart. It was my only chance to see you, before I had to go. Well, I shouldn't say 'had to go,' I want to go. It will be so wonderful to be with your father and my family again, but I want to know you're going to be okay."

Once again, there was a flash of understanding, and Dante saw the kitchen empty, with his mother lying on the ground and Gwen crying beside her. It was then that he truly began to realize what he was experiencing. Still, Dante had always been somewhat of a skeptic, at least in his adult life, so it was hard for him to believe this was anything more than a vision or a dream. Even with everything he'd gone through and learned, Dante felt he had to hold on to some of his old understandings, or he'd risk losing everything and becoming someone completely different.

"I don't want you to go, mom. Everything is changing, and I need you. You raised me by yourself . . . you gave me everything I needed after dad died . . . I'm scared, mom," Dante said, for the first time admitting the fear to himself. "It's not that I am scared of death. I used to face that every day. I'm scared of losing you, Gwen . . . the way my life is . . ."

"Everyone's a little scared of change, sweetheart, but that doesn't always mean it's a bad thing. A little fear is healthy, but remember what I always used to say? 'Don't worry about anything; instead, pray about everything.'"

"That's from Philippians 4:6. I remember. You always used to quote it to me whenever I'd come home from school upset about something," Dante smiled for a second. "But mom, all of this that's about to happen . . . it's real. I don't think memory verses and faith are going to help me now."

"Son, I never tried to push my faith on you, and I'm not going to try now," Becky looked over at the spot on the kitchen floor again. "But my time with you is growing short, and I need to know I've left you with everything I possibly can. Other than you and your father, my faith was all I ever had, and it never failed me . . . just like yours won't fail you."

Dante felt a twinge of shame at the mention of his faith, something he'd allowed himself to lose a long time ago, but there were few people he trusted more than his mother, so maybe there was something to what she was saying.

"I'll try, mom. Why do you have to go? What happened?" Dante reached out to grab her hand, but he felt a strange sensation of beginning to slip away.

"You'll know when the time is right, but for now, all you need to know is that Gwen is going to need you now, more than ever. Not to be strong . . . but to be you," Becky said. "When your father and I found out we were having you . . . it was the happiest we'd ever been. When you were born, we both wanted nothing more than to protect you from all the bad in the world, and right now I wish I could do more to protect you still. I love you so much, Dante. Please . . . never forget that."

"I won't, mom. I love you, too," Dante fought back tears, hoping to hold on to the moment for a little longer. "I will always remember everything you taught me. I am who I am because of your strength. But I still . . . I don't want you to go . . ."

Dante felt like there was something he wasn't saying or something he wasn't seeing. He wasn't sure which, but he felt everything slipping away, so he knew there was no more time to think about it. Whatever this had been, and he truly felt he now knew, it had been a blessing, and he hadn't realized how much he needed a boost until then. He'd been holding everything in and bearing the weight of the world on his shoulders, partially through his own feelings of guilt and worry, but also because he'd allowed John to slowly turn him into something he wasn't. He was more than the choices that he'd made, and he was more than a plan his father and John had concocted thirty years ago.

"I know, dear. I know. But it's time. I've held on too long already, and I don't want to keep your father waiting anymore. Remember what I said, and remember that I'm always with you. We both are. And soon . . . it may seem like your time to join us, but that won't be for a long time," Becky said, standing and walking towards the door. "I love you so much, Gwen, too and . . ."

Dante couldn't make out the end of her sentence, as she opened the door and he was blinded by a bright light, which was accompanied by an odd, melodious sound. He blinked rapidly, trying to see into the light, but he couldn't. The door gently shut behind her, and he was left alone in the darkness, desperately wishing for the light to come back.

CHAPTER 34

DANTE

At the sound of footsteps, Dante shot up from the floor and looked in every direction. He recognized his surroundings and all the training dummies he'd been using, but he had no idea how much time had passed since he'd closed his eyes. As soon as John entered the room, Dante grabbed him by the arm, feeling a sense of urgency he'd not yet felt, even knowing how dangerous the mission was. Realizing he was slightly out of his mind and still partially in the moment with his mother, he let go of John and took a deep, unnecessary breath.

"Gwen . . . is she here?" Dante said, his heart racing.

"She just arrived," John said, seemingly worried. "What's wrong with you? Did you have another vision?"

Dante ignored the question and raced past John to the elevator controls, entering John's codes from memory. Leaving John behind, he allowed the doors to close behind him and headed towards the upper floors to meet his wife. The memory of whatever he'd just experienced with his mother wasn't fading like a normal dream, so he knew there was much more to it than that. In his heart, he knew it was the last time he'd ever get the chance to see and talk to the woman who had raised him alone since he was four years old. Her advice and the verse she'd given to him stayed with him, but most of all, he tried to hold on to the love he felt from that simple and short conversation. More than anything, he felt that it was something he would need to remember in the coming few days.

CHAPTER 35

GWEN

GWEN ROLLED HER EYES AS yet another form was placed in front of her, requiring her signature and several seemingly random yes/no answers about her past and intentions. John had met her at the entrance and explained a few things to her, though knowing him, he'd undoubtedly left out much more than he'd told. Still, she knew that she had to jump through all of the hoops in order to see Dante, even in a secure room in the upper levels. Gwen didn't really care at all about what was going on in the lower levels of the base. She just wanted to have the time to speak with her husband, explain to him what had happened to Becky, and then hopefully watch his face as she told him he was going to be a father. She still hadn't decided if she should explain about his mother or the baby first. Telling him about his mother first would enable the news of the baby to lighten his mood somewhat, but it would also cast a shadow forever on the experience of becoming a father. Gwen felt like there wasn't a right answer, but it gave her some comfort to consider her options as she went about the mind-numbing work of filling out all the forms before her.

As she was flipping through the packet in front of her, Gwen felt a rush of panic as someone ran into the room and grabbed her. It wasn't until she felt the familiar lips on hers that she realized it was Dante. Not even questioning where he'd come from or what they were about to face together, she just held onto him tightly and was glad that she'd gone against his wishes. At some point, she'd have to visit the old Catholic priest and tell him that he'd actually been a help, but being there with Dante, that didn't seem very important to her anymore.

"What . . . you're supposed to wait . . . what . . ." Gwen was more than a little confused, as John had told her it would be another twenty minutes before she was cleared to see Dante. *Clearly, no one told HIM.*

Dante grabbed her by the hand and gently led her out of the lobby and towards a well-guarded, much smaller room. She watched amazed as he pushed past the confused guards and ignored their pleas to stop. When one seemed to reach for his gun, Dante held up his identification and just stared at him until he lowered his head and stepped aside. Dante ushered Gwen through the doors, and then pulled the door shut tightly behind him.

"I'm probably going to hear about that later, but I couldn't wait until you finished those stupid forms," Dante said, hugging her tightly. "So . . . how are your parents? Doing well?"

Gwen knew he was trying to lighten the mood and calm her down a little bit, but she wasn't entirely sure how to answer the question still. Obviously she hadn't gone to visit her parents, but she hadn't really stopped to think about how she was doing. She could really turn him back on his heels and blow his mind by telling him about the baby now, then waiting until a later moment to tell him about his mom, but that didn't feel right to her. She decided to just say whatever came out, and be in the moment as much as she possibly could be in it.

"We both knew I wasn't going to go there and just sit around," Gwen laughed, then sadly looked down. "Dante, I did go visit Becky, though, and there's something I have to tell you . . ."

She was glad that he interrupted her, because she wasn't quite sure how to finish that sentence.

"I know. I'm sorry you had to be there . . . she . . . she loved you like a daughter," Dante said.

For the second time in the last few minutes, Gwen was more confused than she'd ever been. After a second, though, she felt anger rush through her at the thought that John had swooped in and told Dante about his mother, or, worse yet, lied about it and made it seem less serious than she felt it was. She'd always known more about John than she let on, but at the same time, he'd done so much for her and her family, and even Dante, that she chose to just let him be who he claimed to be and leave it at that. It wasn't that she didn't love him, and she knew that he loved her, in his own way, but the more she had to deal with, the more she began to think about him differently. Trust was very important to her, especially now, and she just wasn't sure if she could still say she trusted John.

"Who told you?" Gwen asked, fearing the answer.

"This is going to sound a little unbelievable, but she did."

Gwen looked at him for a moment, wondering if she was missing something. Then she thought about everything that had happened to both of them the last few weeks, and she realized that she could believe just about anything now. In some ways, the news that Dante had somehow talked to his newly deceased mother was among the more believable things that had happened in the last few days.

"Unbelievable kind of has a different meaning now," Gwen said. "I'm so sorry, though. She called me, but I didn't make it in time. I got there and . . ."

Dante pulled her close and gently hugged her. She could feel his heart racing, and she wondered if he was trying to be strong for her, or if he really was this much under control somehow. She'd always loved his ability to lighten the mood while still taking control of any situation, but she'd also seen how much he'd had to deal with the last few weeks, so she wasn't sure how much of this was real and how much of it was a show.

"I know. She's in a better place. She's with dad," Dante said.

Gwen had never in her life heard Dante say anything like that, so she was taken aback by it more than anything else that had happened. She pulled out of the hug and looked into his eyes, partially just to see their bright blue again, but also to check and make sure it was really him. She fought the urge to pinch him, and simply decided to be up front.

"What exactly has happened to you out here?"

Dante laughed, "A lot. We'll get to that later. I learned pretty much everything about my father's death and his last mission from a recording he left, and I found out a great deal about myself and what's to come, but right now, let's just talk about you. Boy or girl?"

Gwen stared at him dumbfounded, unsure of what he was even talking about at first. When she realized he was referring to her pregnancy test, her eyes got very wide, and she had no idea how to respond.

"What . . . I didn't tell anyone. How did . . . what?"

"Let's just say I realized it when I talked with mom," Dante said. "It's hard to explain, and I'll get to all of that. I'm sorry, I should have let you tell me. I'm sure you were working up to that. Here, I'll pretend I don't know. So, Gwen, anything new?"

Gwen was torn between laughing at and hitting Dante, but it had been so long since they'd been together, she was just glad to see him act more like himself again. It had been weeks since he'd cracked a joke or even smiled, with the pain from the headaches and visions tearing through him each time, and she knew the guilt he felt over her worry probably hurt him even more.

"Oh, well, since you asked, I have some news for you . . . are you ready? It's big," Gwen said, barely holding in her laughter.

"I am definitely ready. What's up? New puppy?"

"Close. I'm pregnant," Gwen felt a great deal of anxiety leave her at just saying the words out loud.

"That's amazing," Dante hugged her again, then kissed her lightly on the forehead. "Have you been to a doctor yet? Do we know anything?"

"I just took the test on the day you left, so I haven't really had time to do anything else, especially with all the travel," Gwen said.

"I'll make sure you get checked out here. You know I love you, right?" Dante said.

Gwen was startled by the randomness of the question. Something had clearly happened to shake Dante up, or what he was about to tell her was worse than she'd even imagined. As with any marriage, they'd had a few rocky points, but it had never been anything they'd been unable or unwilling to work through. Because of the early loss of his father, Gwen knew that Dante only used the "l" word when he truly meant it and felt it completely, something she admired and respected about him. For him to say it when she first got there wouldn't have been a surprise, but for him to say it in the midst of a conversation really concerned her.

"Of course. I love you, too. Now . . . tell me a little bit about what's going on with you?"

Gwen shuddered at the sudden change in Dante's demeanor. She knew he was doing his best to "be himself" for her, and also that he was genuinely glad about her being there and the news, but she felt that something was hanging in the air unsaid. Part of her didn't really want to know, because she didn't want anything to ruin this moment for either of them, but, at the same time, she knew she had to get involved somehow, even if it was just listening. She nodded patiently as Dante held up his index finger and walked to the door to speak with one of the guards. After a few minutes of back and forth between him and Dante, and then him and probably John, Dante reentered the room and shut the door behind him. Gwen wanted to ask several specific questions, not the least of which was what had just happened with the guards and even where John was at the moment. However, she knew that he would do his best to answer everything, so she just sat there and gave him the time he needed to gather himself.

"If there's one thing I've learned from having to deal with John's half-truths and manipulations over the years, it's that I'm going to tell you everything I know right now," Dante said. "But I have to warn you, there's a lot of it you're not going to like, especially the upcoming mission."

Gwen felt like her heart stopped at the words "upcoming mission," but she simply nodded her approval and listened, as Dante went through everything he'd learned about himself and the situation over the time since they'd been separated. For the next several minutes, she felt like she wasn't even breathing, as every new thing she learned was even more unbelievable and potentially frightening than the last. When he finally got to the part about his own DNA being different, she reflexively touched her stomach, wondering what the effect would be on their unborn, newly conceived child. That thought never left her mind, even as Dante went through the upcoming mission and the role he had to play. When he was finally finished explaining everything he could, they both sat there, looking at each other. Neither willing to say what she assumed was on both of their minds.

CHAPTER 36

JOHN

John kept a watchful eye on the situation room in the upper level, where Dante was telling Gwen all of their classified secrets. He'd known all along that was going to happen, which partially justified his holding back of several things. He wasn't exactly angry at the interaction between Dante and Gwen, especially since he knew the more Dante shared with her, the more he'd accept from him. Keeping some of his attention on the monitor, John picked up his walkie talkie, making sure it was on his individual secure station.

"What's the status on the teleportation chamber?" John spoke quietly into the walkie talkie.

"It's ahead of schedule, sir. We were able to use the new blueprints to upgrade some of our previous failed designs, and we're optimistic that we will be finished within the next few hours."

"Excellent. Keep me apprised of the situation," John replied. "And remember, as far as Dante and anyone else below my clearance level is concerned, there were no previous versions."

"Understood, sir."

John put away the walkie talkie and went back to studying the monitor. He'd turned down the sound, because he knew the character of Dante would prohibit him from spending too much time trashing anything John had said or done. He watched the situation unfold before him closely, and, through the way Gwen kept holding her stomach and Dante's occasional glances towards it, John realized that there was more to what was going on than even he'd known. For the second time since this began, John once again felt the unfamiliar sensation of guilt over what had to be done. No matter the cost, he knew that his course was clear. Any potential extraterrestrial threat to the earth had to be stopped permanently and forcefully, even if the threat was unintentional and already on the planet. Staring at the monitor, the often-joked about as "missing" heart of CIA Agent John Dawson broke for the second time in his life.

CHAPTER 37

DANTE

Dante sat in the small, quiet room, holding his wife and listening to the sound of her breathing. They'd spent their time together talking about everything. From her horrible experience of finding his mom dead to her ordeal trying to figure out whether or not to come to the base to the fear she had that it would be too late, Gwen had unloaded all of her worries and thoughts, and he hoped it had made her feel better. For his part, he explained everything he could about his experiences with his father's memories and the mission that he was about to attempt. Dante knew Gwen had done her best to understand everything he'd told her, but it was just too much for any sane person to handle, especially all at once after a cross country flight.

After a few laughs and a few more tears, she'd finally fallen asleep on his shoulder. She hadn't been asleep long, and he feared she would wake up the second he moved a muscle, so he just sat, thinking. John had yet to give him a clear answer about very many things, but certain things he had tried to explain struck Dante as wrong, or, at the very least, more incomplete than others. Obviously, Dante wasn't stupid, and he knew that believing there had never been any attempts at preparing for a possible invasion before now were ludicrous. In fact, he was fairly certain that there were probably several protocols in place in case Dante failed, or they failed to account for something. Still, something was off, and he couldn't quite place what it was . . . yet.

"Excuse me, sir," one of the guards assigned to the room stuck his head in cautiously. "Agent Dawson says you're needed in the lower levels. We will stay here and guard Mrs. Smith."

Dante cringed a little bit, but he wasn't sure if it was more from the mention of John's name or the fear that the guard's voice would wake up Gwen.

"Thank you," Dante said, feeling much calmer than the last time he'd had a discussion with the guard. "Give us a few minutes, and I'll head out."

As soon as the guard closed the door behind him, Dante gently shook Gwen to bring her back to reality, such as it was. He hated doing it, but he knew that if he somehow had been able to sneak away with her still asleep, it would be a much greater pain for her to wake up alone with no explanation. The time for his departure was growing very near, Dante could feel that, so he wanted to make things as easy as possible on Gwen. Now that he knew she was pregnant, everything seemed even more important than it had before. It was strange how much even the promise of a new life gave him a renewed sense of hope. At the very least, it meant that she wouldn't be alone if something were to go wrong and he couldn't make it back to her.

"Gwen, sweetheart, I need to go down to the lower levels and work on some final prep with John," Dante said soothingly. "I'll be back to see you before . . . well, I'll be back to see you."

Dante could see Gwen's internal conflict with whether or not it was futile to try and argue for him to stay or for her to be able to go. After a few seconds, she leaned in and kissed him softly on the lips, apparently having reached a decision.

"I understand," Gwen said. "Well, I don't, but it's not about me right now. Be safe and come back to me, okay?"

"Always and forever," Dante stood to leave. "If you need anything, these guards will make sure I get word. Don't hesitate to ask. I'll be back."

Dante hugged his wife one more time, then exited the room. It was far easier to do it all at once than to stretch out their departure, because then he wasn't sure if he'd be able to walk away from her. After leaving explicit instructions with the guards as to what he expected from them, in terms of protecting her and seeing to anything she may need, Dante felt satisfied enough to head to the lower levels. Although the trip was the same distance as always, it seemed much shorter, as everything John had said and done kept swirling around in Dante's head. He knew there was something he was missing, something besides John's apparent overabundance of knowledge about the visions. As he stepped out of the elevator and saw John discussing something with one of the scientists supposedly working on the teleportation device, everything clicked. *But I need to be sure.*

"Dante, there is a lot we need to discuss," John shooed away the scientist, apparently finished with whatever it was they were talking about and didn't want Dante to hear the rest.

"That's the first thing we've agreed about in quite a while, John," Dante followed him through the doors into a small, private chamber with a table and two chairs, but apparently nothing else. "Why don't you start?"

Dante smirked a little bit at the confused stare John gave. It was nice to be the one on the vague end of things for once, but it was true that he probably needed to focus on whatever it was John had prepared to discuss. For once, he felt like he had something on John. Just thinking that, though, was kind of a shock to Dante. When they'd first met, he'd felt a lot of resentment and anger towards John, but over the years, they'd grown a strong friendship. It was strange for him to question all of that now, even though he knew it was more than justified because of everything he'd learned, and even more so because of what he knew he'd yet to learn.

"Very well. I'm going to place all of my cards on the table, Dante. We need to discuss your abilities and how far they've progressed. Obviously, I know a little more than I've told you. I probably know even more than Conner had surmised before his death," John cringed at the mention of Conner's death, something that wasn't lost on Dante. "I knew you'd have a flash during the recording, because I placed subliminal test phrases into it after we realized you had begun having visions in the first place."

"I'm sure there's more, but why don't you get to the point. What do you want to know about my 'abilities'?" Dante sat back calmly, knowing John was using one of his old tricks at manipulating a situation.

"Yes, well, simply put, we've always believed that, once the visions began to manifest, then other mental abilities should follow closely. Perhaps even the ability to control the visions," John said. "Look, I'm sure you're about sick of this, so let me cut to the chase. We want . . . I want you to try to focus, see if you can go inside the vision, maybe make contact with . . . well, with your 'brother.'"

Dante shivered at the notion that the leader of the creatures had any genetic connection to him, but he knew that it was true, or at least he knew that his father had believed it to be true.

"Let's not call him that, not until we know more about what's happening up there," Dante said. "What are you expecting here? Do you want me to just meditate and chant and then boom . . . my mind is flying through space? I have no idea how to control these things . . ."

"Did you have an encounter with your mother earlier?" John asked, looking down at the table.

Dante stood up and calmly walked over to John, then grabbed him by the lapels and slammed him against the closest wall. Even in his agitated state, he had enough control of himself to keep from hurting John. In fact, he wasn't even any angrier than he'd been before, but he hoped that John wouldn't know that. After all, sometimes a little fear was good for the soul.

"I was asleep. How did you know that?" Dante yelled, no longer caring who heard. "What else aren't you telling me, John? Who else is going to have to die in order to finish this thing you started 30 years ago?"

As he held John against the wall, two things seemed strange to him. First, John hadn't struggled at all. Dante wasn't sure if that meant he'd expected it or if he just knew how strong Dante was and didn't see any need in expending any energy for a futile escape attempt. The second thing, though was more troubling. Even though the number of people on the lower levels was much lower than the upper levels, there had to be someone nearby that had heard either the noise of someone being slammed against a wall or Dante's yelling. As he noticed a trickle of sweat escape from John's forehead, Dante could see that John had been wondering the same thing. Thinking about this new development almost caused him to miss John's response, as he wondered whether something else was going on to keep everyone's attention on the base or simply no one cared what happened anymore.

"We have developed a device that lets us track your mental activity, so yes, I know most of what happens in each of your visions. I can tell, for the most part, when they're about to happen, and I knew you had an encounter earlier that was unlike anything else we'd seen," John, for his part, stayed calm. "In fact, that's why we believe you're growing in your abilities and may be able to control it enough to give us a greater idea of what's coming towards us. I know you're unhappy with me, but this is about more than your hurt feelings, Dante. You want me to be real? Your father gave his life for this project, and the least you can do is sit down and try this out. When we're done, then you can beat any answers you want out of me. Until then, I'm in charge."

Even though Dante was, in fact, a little angry and even questioned the sincerity of John's harsh comments, he knew it was the truth. Granted it was his life that was being messed up the most, everyone else had a high stake in this mission, and if it didn't work out, there was no telling how far the devastation would go. Dante let John go, then walked back to his seat and sat down quietly and, without a word, closed his eyes and tried to picture the last vision he'd had of the inside of the spacecraft.

After several minutes of trying to no avail, Dante finally felt like he was making some progress. He tried to focus on the few images of his "brother" that he had glimpsed thus far, feeling that the unfortunate but likely genetic connection they shared would provide him the best chance at making some kind of connection. For an instant, he felt it click into place. He felt all of the hatred and pain coming from his brother's mind, and he knew without a doubt that this man had to be referred to as his brother now. He saw everything that his brother saw. He could see an army of alien creatures methodically walking around the ship, all of which seemed to be trying to avoid any kind of unnecessary contact with their leader. Dante watched through his brother's eyes as his ship soared through space in a vector he assumed was unknown by humans, but he could tell that the ship was always moving, which meant they were on their way. Tensing up, his brother moved calmly and quickly towards one of the reflective surfaces that seemingly lined the ships inner walls. Dante strained to get a glimpse of a face or of any distinguishing characteristics, but his brother had apparently shut his eyes. It was such a simple tactic, but also a very effective one, and it left Dante completely blind while he was in his brother's mind. There was only blackness and silence, until he heard the same voice that had threatened him earlier, as well as gave out the orders of invasion to his apparent alien subjects.

"Soon."

It started as a whisper and grew louder, shaking Dante back to his own body once again. Dante opened his eyes and could feel the fear flowing through every part of his body. He almost fell over as he tried to stand up. He hobbled over to John, who struggled to help Dante regain his balance. This had taken almost as much out of him as all his other visions, maybe even more. Dante feared that it was more from his brother's impact than the use of some new mental ability he was unsure how to work properly.

"What happened? Did it work?" John's voice was frantic, half through the thrill of general scientific curiosity and half through apparent concern for once.

"I was . . . I was him. I saw through his eyes . . . I could tell what he was thinking . . . what he was feeling. So much hatred . . . so much pain . . ."

Dante collapsed to the floor, still conscious, but feeling absolutely no strength at the moment. He'd definitely learned that he could control aspects of his mind, but it took a great deal out of him. Especially since his brother undoubtedly had the same, or perhaps greater, abilities as Dante.

"Dante, you've got to calm down. You've got to remember exactly what happened. Did you find out anything?" John said. "If you really made contact, then it's vital you tell me everything."

Dante rubbed his hands over his eyes and slowly stood up, attempting to fully regain his composure. He toyed with the idea of telling John to just go check the devices they had trained on Dante's mind, but he knew it wasn't the time for selfish anger. Everything had gotten much more serious now, but for some reason, it still didn't seem very real. Dante wondered idly if that was a side effect of everything that had happened or if more was going on than he knew.

"Okay . . . I think . . . I think I can handle it all now. It was just so intense, being in someone else's thoughts. I couldn't find out anything exact about when they will arrive, but just before I was forced out of his mind, he said . . . he just said 'soon.' He knew I was there. He's a step ahead of us, John. Probably more than a step. They're coming."

INTERLUDE

Ulysses quietly shut the door to his chamber and walked slowly and confidently towards the alien creature manning the main controls.

"I trust we are on schedule with the opening of the warp gate," he said with a threatening stare at the trembling creature, who responded with a series of clicks and strange noises seemingly coming from the back of his throat.

"Excellent. We will give them what they expect, just not exactly how they expect it."

His laughter was soon cut off by a second alien creature that emerged from a path leading to the main section of the ship. The creatures made similar noises, which were also met by laughter from Dante's brother.

"No, that will not be necessary. I want him to teleport aboard the ship unharmed. Yes, I look forward to seeing the look on his face when he realizes that he is too late to stop the invasion. Prepare the forces now," he turned once again to the alien creature manning the main controls. "Make the final necessary calculations and prepare the ship for warp. It's not quite time yet, but the time is growing very near. Very near, indeed."

* * *

CHAPTER 38

GWEN

GWEN SHIVERED AS A COLD chill ran down her spine. Her grandmother had always told her that meant someone had stepped on her grave, and it was only now that Gwen actually realized how morbid that little saying truly had been.

"Ma'am, do you need anything else?"

Gwen smiled at the guard that seemingly checked on her every few minutes. Whatever Dante had said to them had apparently had quite an effect, as they'd hustled to bring her food, magazines, and even a small TV/DVD combo, although she had no interest in really being entertained at the moment.

"No, I'm doing fine, thank you," Gwen said. "I appreciate everything you've done, but . . . do you have any idea when Dante or John may be heading up here again?"

"No, ma'am. Honestly, we probably know less than you at this point," the guard added, then popped back out to join his fellow servicemen.

She wasn't exactly worried, not any more than any normal person would be, but Gwen couldn't shake the feeling that something bad was about to happen. She just wasn't sure if it was a motherly or wifely feeling of dread, but either way, she didn't like it. Checking her watch for the fifth time in the last five minutes, she grabbed another magazine and tried to trick herself into thinking about something else for a while. After all, if anything big was about to happen, she was sure Dante would find a way to get to her.

CHAPTER 39

JOHN

John left Dante alone for a few minutes to gather himself, deciding to take the opportunity to check on the progress of the teleportation device. The fact that Dante's powers had grown significantly had proven to be a bittersweet deal for John, as it was good to know, but meant their time was growing very short. It was everything he could do to not run down the hall and through the corridor to where the final preparations were being made.

"Status update?" John asked as he entered the room, not caring who answered.

"We are basically prepared for the first test, but even if that's successful, there's still a lot of work to do. The possibility of a return trip alone . . ." one of the scientists answered.

"That's not a priority," John said. "Our mission is to send Dante to infiltrate the main ship and try to do as much damage as possible before they invade. As long as that's accomplished, nothing else matters. We'll worry about a return trip once the mission is deemed successful."

John ignored the looks he was getting from several of the scientists. There was no time for tact, and he felt like he was the only one working to get through all of this successfully. He knew what the creatures had been capable of even before they'd gotten a leader to focus their attacks and invasions. As much as he truly looked at Dante as a son, John still believed that the possible sacrifice of one far outweighed the deaths of thousands, or possibly even millions, depending on how fast or effective the government's response team would be in an invasion. He'd already notified his superiors of what was going on, so he took solace in the fact that he wasn't the only one currently stressed with preparation.

"Understood, sir. We'll test it immediately. After that, I suppose it will be ready for Mr. Smith at your discretion," the scientist replied.

"See that it is," John said. "When the time comes, we won't have the luxury of waiting around for tests or proper procedures, unfortunately. This is about our planet's survival, so please keep that in mind."

John stood, watching the scientists work at continuing to prepare the teleportation device. He could see Dante's sword and the two metallic boxes on a desk nearby, and he hoped that they worked as well as Conner and he had planned all those years ago.

INTERLUDE

"What makes you think this has any chance of working, John?" Conner asked. "Won't the EMP knock out the nuke?"

Conner hated all of this. He hated the secrecy and the thought of a possible invasion. He hated having to trust John with something so important as his son's life, but most of all, he hated being away from Becky and Dante any more than he had to be, especially now.

"In a technical sense, it's not a nuke, Conner. It will have virtually the same impact, but it doesn't have near the radioactive fallout of a typical nuclear bomb," John said. "We'll be placing it within a special metal casing that should reflect the blast of the EMP, rather than allow it inside. Trust me, I have just as much riding on this as you."

Conner glared at John, feeling all of his frustrations and fears welling up inside of him at John's last comment. This was his son's life they were talking about, and although the events they were planning for may never happen, there was nothing Conner hated more than the thought of a world without Dante. Although every childbirth is considered a miracle, Conner had seen a special significance in Dante's birth. It was a sign that everything Conner had gone through had been worth it. Even though he'd had to deal with tremendous pain, he'd been given a chance to heal, simply by bringing a new life into the world and loving it.

"No, you don't. You never will," Conner whispered, mostly to himself, then raised his voice to reply. "Fine, I suppose that makes sense. Well, as much as any of this does. Planning for something that may never happen . . . John, we should just put together a force and go take them out now, while they're not expecting it. The more time we give them . . ."

"Using what, Conner? You've seen the warp drive tests. Nothing's worked since you came back. Unless they're hovering around the moon, or maybe even Mars, we've got no realistic way of reaching them," John replied.

Conner shook his head and picked up the sword they'd created using the alien metal they'd found earlier. Although he understood the thought behind using a sword against the seemingly projectile-geared forcefields, it still seemed odd to him that such an old style of weapon would be effective against such an advanced race. In a way it made some kind of sense, he supposed. The idea of the Kevlar vest being vulnerable to a knife, of course, had been the basis of their thought process, but it just seemed like such a shot in the dark. Conner prayed that they'd never have to face the threat of an invasion. He'd seen firsthand what the creatures were capable of, and he desperately wanted his son to have no part of any of this. Still, something kept nagging at him, an inner voice that kept telling him he had no choice in the matter. They were coming, and there was nothing Conner could do to stop it.

"We're almost done here, is it okay if I head home? I promised Becky I'd do my best to be back before she put Dante to bed," Conner felt a growing sense of dread, but he was unable to figure out why.

"As soon as you make that recording for Dante," John said, tilting his head slightly in confusion. "I thought you were adamant that we lock everything up before you left? Not that I'd mind if you changed your mind. It makes much more sense to work on all of this now . . . perfect it over the years. Be ready."

Conner blinked rapidly, feeling a strong headache building. It wasn't like him to forget things, much less important things like making sure John and the government didn't have any weapons or materials they wouldn't necessarily need.

"No . . . you're right. We need to get that done," Conner grabbed the recorder and the teleportation plans. "Let's get that taken care of now. I'm not feeling so hot, and I'd really like to get home before this headache has a chance to run its course."

"Of course," John said, picking up the remaining materials they planned on locking up. "Would you like me to get you some medication before we continue?"

"No, I'll be fine. Let's just get going. It's getting dark, and Becky will be worried if I'm not back, soon," Conner said. "John, I know you've had some issues playing it straight with me in the past, but I really need to be able to trust you with all of this. I don't care how much you disagree, but this is my son . . . my life . . . my family. This has to be done my way or not at all. Please."

When John didn't reply, Conner began to wonder if he'd even said anything out loud. The headache was growing, and he wasn't even sure if he'd be able to get through the recording, much less drive home. Still, for Dante's sake, he had to try. When they reached their destination without any reply from John, Conner began to repeat himself, but John placed a hand on his shoulder and stopped him.

"We may never see eye to eye on how things should be done," John said. "But I will respect your wishes on this. What happened to you and Gre . . . Officer Williams was a travesty, and it's the least I can do to honor you both."

Satisfied with John's reply, Conner sat down and pressed the record button. He'd been thinking about what to say the entire time they'd been working, so he felt confident that he wouldn't miss a beat now, headache or not. As he was speaking into the device, he managed to put all the pain and worry aside, and instead just pretended like he was looking at his son across the table. He imagined what he'd look like in ten years, twenty years, even thirty years, and he hoped that he'd be around to see it. Once the recording was finished, Conner and John carried everything to the specified location and locked it. Conner made sure that everything was in order, just as he'd been promised and, satisfied started to head out of the room. Before he took two steps, though, he clutched his head in agony and fell to the ground.

* * *

CHAPTER 40

DANTE

DANTE SLOWLY RUBBED THE SIDES of his head, trying to rid himself of the headache he'd gotten by stretching his mind so far. When John came in, he knew that everything was almost ready. The closer he got to the time of his departure, the less real everything seemed to him. The idea that at some point in the next hour, it was likely he wouldn't be on earth anymore baffled him. Everything that had happened had seemingly prepared him for this, but still, Dante just couldn't completely grasp the concept. He understood the plan, as it had been described to him, but there was still something John was holding back. Because of the gravity of the situation, he wasn't sure whether or not to bring it up. Dante didn't care so much about John's feelings on the matter, but he felt that if he could keep it to himself, then perhaps he'd be able to figure everything out without John's interference.

"Feeling any better, Dante?" John said, casually sitting down across from him.

"I'm fine. What's the schedule look like?" Dante replied.

"Everything's ready. As soon as we have confirmation of alien arrival, we will be able to use the nearest satellite to pinpoint the location of the main ship and teleport you aboard," John said.

"You understand how crazy that all sounds, right? I mean . . . taking out the fact that teleportation is mostly known from Star Trek, then you've still got the fact that I'm going in blind . . . to outer space. Blind. What are the chances this will even work? Be honest, for once." Dante said.

Dante watched as John seemed to calculate exactly what to say in his head. Whereas usually, John would always weigh his options of which answer would benefit him the most, Dante actually felt that this time, he was just trying to say something unpleasant. He was torn between being comforted that John was probably going to tell him the truth and feeling the normal discomfort with finding out that his odds weren't all that great.

"From a mathematical standpoint, the odds are very low. Even if everything goes perfectly, there's no guarantee the ship won't simply move out of the way at the last minute," John paused. "However, too much has happened for me to believe that they don't have their own plan. If they wanted to invade, they could have done so at any point over the last 30 years, and we'd have been ill equipped to even pretend to mount a defense. So, logically, I believe whoever is in charge is going to allow you to board safely."

Dante hadn't expected that as an answer, but it made a certain amount of sense to him. If the alien leader truly was some kind of a brother to him, then the odds were that he wanted to have a personal confrontation. The fact that all of this seemed somewhat logical to Dante frightened him, as he probably would have changed the channel if he'd seen a similar plot in a science fiction movie on TV.

"So what you're saying is that we expect the plan to work, because they're expecting the plan? So . . . what's the point? What's to stop them from just surrounding me when I get there, taking my weapons and the bombs, and then just invading anyway?" Dante asked.

"Nothing. However, knowing that we are planning something isn't the same as knowing what we are planning. We have no idea what kind of technology they have, other than what we've learned from your visions or Conner's experiences. By the same token, they have a limited understanding of what we are capable of as a technological race. From the way they easily took care of Conner and Gre . . . Conner and Officer Williams, we have to assume they'll be overconfident," John said.

"That's a lot to assume, but I suppose we don't have any other options" Dante said, rubbing his goatee and thinking things through. "I want Gwen brought down here. Now. I don't care what strings you have to pull or how much red tape you have to cut. This is the safest place in the world, and I'm not leaving her to chance."

"Done," John said. "In fact, I'll go take care of it myself now. Why don't you go and familiarize yourself with the layout of the ship, from Conner's perspective, again?"

"Sure . . . I . . . I'll go do that. Thanks." Dante said, confused.

Since John had never agreed to something so quickly, Dante had no idea what he had planned. The fact that John and Gwen had a familial relationship at least put Dante's worries about her safety to rest, but there had to be a reason John was so willing to bypass security clearance and bring Gwen deeper into the base. However, since it meant knowing that Gwen was as safe as she possibly could be, he simply didn't care to find out.

CHAPTER 41

JOHN

JOHN STOOD AT THE DOOR, watching his niece sit and pretend to read, though the fact that she kept checking her cell phone every two minutes gave away that her focus wasn't in the magazine. He'd already sent the men assigned to protect her out to guard the front gates, just in case. At the very least, it enabled them to keep up appearances that it was just a normal day. Looking at Gwendolyn, the only family he'd truly been able to call his own, John wondered what the next few hours and days would be like for her. Even if everything went perfectly, he knew the chances of Dante's return were very small, and if things went poorly, then there was a good chance none of them would be leaving that base for a long time. Putting those thoughts aside for the moment, John pushed open the door and walked in to sit down next to Gwendolyn.

"Dante has requested that you be brought down to the lower level," John said. "I have to say, I feel that he's right. We don't know what's going to happen when . . . they arrive."

"What exactly did he have to promise you to get your consent on this, Uncle John?" Gwen continued looking from her magazine to her cell phone, not looking towards John.

"Nothing. I know there have been some questions about my motives lately, but you're my family. I'd do anything to keep you safe, believe me. Anything at all," John replied.

Gwen placed the magazine down and stared into John's eyes, seemingly trying to see through to his soul and discern his true motives. John hated that it was like this between them, but he understood. As far as she was concerned, the only things that mattered now were her husband's life and the life of her unborn child.

"I don't," Gwen stood up. "But I do trust Dante, and if he's about to leave, I want to be there. Let's go."

John started to plead the case for more understanding of his motives, but he was cut off by a frantic voice coming through his walkie talkie. Already knowing what was going on, he picked it up and tried his best to appear calm to the scientist that had called him.

"Is it time?" John stood up and joined Gwendolyn at the door.

". . . . feedback . . . . satellite imaging just . . . device ready . . . time is of the . . . NOW!" came the garbled reply.

John put his walkie talkie away and gently grabbed Gwendolyn by the hand, leading her towards the elevator. There were no words he could say to make her completely understand, but he could at least do his best to get her down to Dante before his departure. Even though John had no regrets about the mission and what was to come, he still cared what Gwendolyn thought, and what she would think if Dante left without saying goodbye. Quickly inputting his secret code, John led Gwendolyn through the doors of the elevator and pressed the buttons to take them to the final leg of their journey.

CHAPTER 42

DANTE

DANTE COULD SENSE THE ANGST and fear of the scientists down the hall even before he heard their frantic yelling about the arrival. He didn't need John or anyone else involved to tell him what this meant. Running towards the lab where he knew they'd built the teleportation device, Dante wondered if John would come through on his promise to bring Gwen down to the lower levels. Even if they didn't make it in time, he wanted to know, more than anything, that she was safe. Shaking those thoughts from his head for the moment, Dante raced into the lab and immediately stopped. Although he'd seen the plans for the teleportation device, it was still an amazing thing to see such a technological marvel complete and operational in front of him. The base was simple enough, some type of metal, which Dante assumed would turn out to be similar to his sword. The actual transportation device was oval in shape and just slightly larger than Dante himself. Even though it hadn't been completely powered up, there was already a shimmering type of effect beginning to swirl from the inner edges of the oval.

"Sir, you need to take a look at this," a scientist handed Dante a tablet computer displaying the satellite reading. "I think it's time to make the final preparations. It may even be past time. The ships seem to have stopped, directly between the earth and the moon, but there's no telling how long they'll stay still. There's some kind of feedback, and we've lost contact with Agent Dawson."

Dante briefly looked back to the entrance of the lab behind him, wondering where exactly John and Gwen were, then decided he had no choice. With the expansion of his mental powers, it was entirely possible he'd be able to contact Gwen from anywhere, and as much as John had gotten under his skin lately, Dante knew he'd do anything to protect Gwen.

"Set the device to ready," Dante said.

"Sir, what about . . ." the scientist replied.

"Just do it," Dante knew the longer he put this off, the harder it would be.

As the scientist went about his final prep work, Dante walked to the nearby table that held everything he'd need for his mission. He sheathed the sword and attached it to a special holder they'd given him to wear on his back, then checked his revolver to make sure it was full. Forcefields or not, Dante had no intention of trusting everything to a sword. At the very least, the EMP should knock out the shields of any creatures he'd run into on board the ship. Placing the two metal boxes containing the bombs carefully into a duffel bag, Dante wondered whether he or the plan would prove to be the craziest. Before he had a chance to think more on the topic, all the power went off, including the teleportation device.

"Power outage is base wide," someone yelled from the doorway to the room.

For a moment, Dante clung to the hope that it was John, but he knew it was just a scientist or soldier that had been out of the room. Deciding it was time to push himself again, Dante reached out with his mind to try to make contact with Gwen. Nearly as soon as his mind touched hers, he lost the connection, but it was enough to let him know they were safely in the elevator on the way to the base, although stuck at the moment due to the power outage. As he was about to attempt a stronger connection, Dante's train of thought was derailed by the sound and image of the teleportation device springing to life at full power.

"How did you do that?" Dante asked, not caring who answered.

"We . . . we didn't. Power's still out . . . it shouldn't be working," the scientist from before replied, obviously scared. "Sir, we shouldn't proceed until . . ."

"I don't think there is an 'until,'" Dante cut him off and headed towards the teleportation device. "It's obvious we're not the only ones with a plan here, and I don't think the power outage was an accident. Make sure Gwen's safe."

With that, Dante took a deep breath and stepped onto the base of the teleportation device. This close, the swirling lights were truly an amazing sight to see, though in a few seconds, he knew they'd pale in comparison to everything else he was about to witness.

"Sir, don't you need . . . shouldn't you be wearing a spacesuit? It's set to teleport you to the largest ship on radar, but . . . if it moves . . . or . . ."

"A suit's not going to save me from being stuck in space or teleported in the middle of a wall," Dante said. "Besides, he wants me alive."

Before the scientist had a chance to question his cryptic response, Dante stepped through the portal in the center of the teleportation device. He truly regretted not being able to say goodbye to Gwen, but he was going to do everything he could to make sure his child wouldn't have to grow up without a father as he had.

* * *

INTERLUDE

“He’s coming. Send the invasion force through the portal now. I only want a small force to stay behind. I don’t want him to accomplish his goal of finding me too easily. After all, he has to prove himself worthy of my time.” Ulysses said calmly. “I want twenty of you to lock onto their teleporter’s signal and head to their base.”

The alien creature at the main controls clicked a few noises and pressed some buttons as a great multitude of others similar to it entered the room. After a few more clicking noises between the apparent commander of the forces and the creature at the controls, several portals in each of the thirty ships opened and the invasion force began to silently step through.

CHAPTER 43

DANTE

SECONDS AFTER STEPPING THROUGH THE teleportation portal, Dante emerged in what appeared to be a docking bay of an incredibly huge spaceship. He closed his eyes and, whispering a small prayer, something that somehow felt right now, removed the sword from its sheath. Carefully, he looked around to make sure he was alone in this area of the ship. Once he felt as secure as he could on an alien spaceship, he closed his eyes and tried to mentally contact John or Gwen. Just like before, he felt like he briefly made a connection which was then immediately ended. It was clear that it wasn't a coincidence, and more than likely wasn't because of anything he was doing wrong. Something troubled him, though. He could tell they were still trapped in the elevator, but there was an abnormal sense of fear and confusion coming from John, something he definitely never expected. Unfortunately he didn't have time to delve any further to try to see what was happening, because three of the alien creatures he had seen in his visions entered the room and began to look around. Dante stepped back, allowing the shadows to engulf him, and watched as the alien creatures split up and searched the area.

Dante carefully placed the duffle bag behind some machinery and remained almost completely immobile until one of the aliens came within a few feet of his position. The alien moved his head around in a fashion that made Dante assume he was about to be discovered. He waited until the alien turned around and then reached out and pulled it back into the shadows with him. Silently, he twirled the creature around so he could look into its eyes, and then quickly rammed his sword through its throat. The alien clutched the wound and fell to the ground in a heap. *Apparently it works. Thanks, dad.* Dante reached down and removed a metallic wristband from the alien, hoping that he was correct in guessing what it was. Pushing a small button on the side of it, he felt a small shock and dropped it to the ground. His jaw dropped momentarily as a small circular forcefield prevented the wristband from touching the ground. He reached down and, applying a small amount of force, managed to reach through the forcefield and once again push the button. Unfortunately, the noise from the forcefield activating was enough to draw the other two alien creatures' attention towards him.

"Well, when in Rome . . ." Dante's whispered as he picked up the wristband, placed it on his wrist and once more pushed the button to activate the forcefield, which clung to his body like a second layer of skin.

Nearly as soon as he triggered the forcefield, the two creatures were upon him, clawing and clicking in a tangled web of limbs, knocking him to the ground. The forcefield seemed to be strong enough to withstand the brunt of their attacks, but it still hurt. One of the creatures had pinned his arm in an awkward position, causing him to be unable to lift the sword with any kind of force. With the other, though, he was able to punch at the creature with enough force to draw his sword and slice it through the sternum, or at least what would be called a sternum on a human. At the sight of its two comrades dying before him, the third alien kicked at Dante and attempted to run out of the room. Using the opportunity to try something he'd wondered about, Dante reached out to the creature's mind. After a moment, the creature stopped, standing unnaturally still just before the doorway. Dante walked over and looked into its eyes, wondering if the creatures aged differently than humans. If so, it was possible this creature could have been one of the ones responsible for what happened to his father and Greta on their mission. Despite a feeling of anger coursing through him, Dante refused to kill the creature in cold blood, removing his mental presence and allowing it to swing wildly at him. Dante was able to easily avoid its clumsy attack and finish the creature off with a quick series of jabs with his sword.

Grabbing the duffle bag and leaving the room, Dante felt a sense of dread at the fact that no other creatures had joined the fray after all the commotion. He looked around and saw no sign of life and continued down the next hallway until he reached what seemed to be a control room. Dante leapt up to grab onto a higher platform and pulled himself up. He squatted low, planning a course of action, as six more aliens sat or stood at various stations in the room, all watching the monitors in front of them and clicking to themselves. Dante quietly hung the duffle bag off of the platform and jumped to an area with three and quickly sliced through them, as the surprise of him interrupting whatever it was they had been doing on the monitors was enough to give him an advantage. Two of the remaining creatures left their stations and leapt at Dante. Though he dodged one, the other was able to knock the sword away from him as it passed. Before he had a chance to grab for it, the other creature that he'd dodged was back on the attack. This time the force of its claw strike was able to tear through the force field, slicing across Dante's chest. Though the pain was excruciating, it seemed to be no more than a surface wound.

Dante spun around, knocking the creature down with a well-placed roundhouse kick to the forehead, and then dodged a claw strike by the second alien. Dante wondered why the third hadn't left his monitor to join the fight, but also why none of the creatures had attempted to pick up his sword. Rolling away, Dante grabbed the sword and swung back at the leaping alien, slicing through its throat and sending it tumbling to the ground in a pool of black blood. Before he had a chance to do likewise to the other creature, it quickly hit a few buttons on a nearby control pad and leaped through a portal that appeared next to it, disappearing just as quickly as it had appeared. Though he didn't like what that could mean, Dante turned his attention to the final alien in the room, which was still sitting at the monitor, not even looking in Dante's direction. Finally looking at the monitor himself, Dante nearly dropped his sword.

On the creature's monitor were several apparently live screenshots of devastation being caused by the invasion around the world. Focusing on the small picture of the base where he'd left Gwen, Dante disregarded his "no killing in cold blood" rule and sliced through the creature at the monitor, wanting to end it as quickly as possible. Trying once more to contact Gwen or John, Dante felt a greater force blocking him. Realizing immediately what this meant, he turned around and jumped back up to the platform where he'd hung the duffel bag, only to discover that it was gone.

CHAPTER 44

JOHN

JOHN COULD HEAR THE SCREAMS through the elevator doors, and he knew what they meant. Not only had the invasion begun, but somehow they'd already infiltrated the base. Wondering if Dante had managed to get through the portal in time, John suddenly felt like a fool.

"They tracked it. Of course . . . I should have planned for this . . ." John muttered.

"John, what's happening? Where's Dante?" Gwen said, barely holding it together.

At the sound of her voice, John snapped back into the moment and looked around the elevator. From the sounds on the other side, it seemed like they were close to the bottom floor, so if he could pry the door open they'd be able to exit into the lower levels. However, it was obvious that, especially in Gwendolyn's condition, that probably wasn't the best course of action.

"Dante's fine. He was able to teleport out before the power went out. The invasion started before we had a chance to get back to him," John said, hoping at least some of what he said was true.

Ignoring anything she may have said in reply, John continued looking around the elevator, hoping something would clear his mind enough to come up with a better plan. Before he had a chance, though, the power came back on and the elevator finished the remainder of its journey to the bottom floor. Quickly slamming his hand into the red button on the elevator's control panel, John stopped its descent before the doors could open. Hearing claws on the door, though, he knew he was already too late. John looked over at his niece and then down at her stomach, where both of her hands currently rested, subconsciously protecting the life growing within her. There weren't many options remaining for him, at least without putting Gwendolyn in more danger than she was currently. If they went back up to the top levels, one or more creatures would no doubt follow through the elevator shaft. If he opened the gates, there'd be no time to protect her and the baby. Although he hadn't yet decided if the unborn child of a genetic case like Dante would be a danger, he couldn't bring himself to put his only family in immediate danger. Closing his eyes and picturing Greta, he reached over and took the panel off the elevator's controls and input a series of commands on the small keypad underneath.

"Gwendolyn . . . whatever happens, don't leave this elevator," John said, removing his gun from its holster and gently shoving her back as he stepped up to the door.

"John . . ." Gwen's sobs showed that she clearly understood what he was planning.

John nodded to her and manually opened the door, firing directly into the creature's face that appeared in front of him as he exited. The bullets wouldn't do any good, but the surprise of the attack followed by the force of the close range firing at least would knock it back so he could allow the doors to close behind him. If he'd configured everything correctly, the elevator would stop just below the main level and stay there until one of the guards input the proper codes to bring it all the way up and open the doors. All John had to do was stay alive long enough to contact them.

CHAPTER 45

DANTE

SINCE THE DUFFLE BAG WAS nowhere to be seen, Dante had no choice but to continue down the upper platform, hoping to find whatever or whoever had grabbed it before they did anything to ruin the plan. Moving through another passageway, he was now in a much larger room with twice as much equipment. There were no aliens in sight, but in the center of the room sat another control panel in front of a large three-dimensional screen and next to a machine that looked startlingly familiar to the teleportation device on Earth. As Dante quietly crept forward, he was interrupted by a loud noise. He turned slowly and was taken aback at what he saw. Half-expecting to see another alien, he was woefully unprepared to gaze upon the face of his "brother." The man he was now locking eyes with was slightly taller than Dante with a more muscular build. The frightening part, though, was that he looked almost identical to Dante's memory of his father, with the main difference being his eerie cold black, pupilless eyes. He was clad in all black, except for a pair of red gloves, one of which was holding Dante's duffle bag. Dante lowered his sword and made a move towards him.

"Who are you?" Dante asked, vainly attempting to mask the fear he was feeling.

The man's scruffy face pulled back into a smile, and he took a step forward to meet Dante's.

"I believe you already know who I am, Dante."

"My brother."

A palpable silence filled the room, as both men simply stood and stared at each other. Dante hoped to keep him talking long enough to figure out a way to get the bag away from him and carry through with his mission. There was no doubt in his mind that one of them wasn't going to be walking away, though.

"I suppose that's true enough. Which version of the story do you know, though, Dante? I can see by the weapon in your hand that father received my little gift. You see, while you were growing at a normal rate, my age was induced and then halted." He looked at Dante's sword and laughed. "My name, in your language, is Ulysses. Quite ironic, isn't it? Both of us named after men who took great journeys. Some would say we were bred to be examples to our races."

"Examples? You're not an example to your race. You're trying to butcher it." Dante was beginning to feel the adrenaline once again pumping through his body. "You are nothing but a murderer in the name of an alien race of which you're not even a true part."

"Don't fool yourself, brother. I am just as much a part of this race as you are of the human race. We are above all and owe nothing to any. I am no more a murderer for destroying lesser beings than you are for stepping on a common insect."

"That's crazy. You're wiping out entire races of beings that are just like you, just like me. They're capable of feeling and reasoning. Can't you see that?" Dante pointed his sword towards Ulysses. "I understand what you must have gone through, not having a family, but you can't keep doing this. I won't let you keep doing this . . ."

Dante's words were cut off by the sharp laughter of Ulysses. Completely without warning, Ulysses looked down at the bag and then tossed it to Dante.

"I believe you'll find these in still working order, but you may not want to use them after I tell you the truth about our father and your friend, John Dawson," Ulysses said. "We share much of the same DNA, so I know you've at least got the potential to intelligently discern the facts from the fiction."

"I'd be much more likely to give you the benefit of the doubt if there wasn't currently an invasion destroying my home and endangering my wife," Dante said, clutching the sword tightly with one hand and the duffle bag with the other.

"Fair point," Ulysses reached to the side and pressed a button on the control panel. "Halt the invasion for now. You may only defend yourselves, no unnecessary attacking. There, Dante . . . that should do it."

"Do you expect me to believe . . ."

"See for yourself," Ulysses said, pulling up the series of live images on the monitor, all of which showed the aliens simply standing at formation for the time being.

* * *

CHAPTER 46

JOHN

JOHN HAD NO IDEA WHY the aliens had stopped attacking, but he took the opportunity to quickly notify the guards on the upper level of Gwen's situation. With that done, he decided to try to make his way to the teleportation device to see if any of the scientists were still alive or if Dante had even began his mission. Half expecting the aliens to stop him, John was surprised that they merely stood aside for him to walk past, with one of them following him. He wasn't able to do an accurate count, but it seemed like there were only twenty or thirty on the base. If they could get rid of the forcefields, the soldiers on hand upstairs should be able to take care of business. Walking into the room with the teleportation device, John was pleased to see that all of the scientists were huddled in a corner, uninjured for the most part, just scared and unsure what to do. It was then that the good news gave way to the bad, as John looked away from the scientists and realized that the teleportation device had been completely, irreparably destroyed.

CHAPTER 47

DANTE

"If you don't believe the images, I'll allow you a moment to contact John, and only John," Ulysses said.

Dante wasn't surprised at the revelation that Ulysses had been behind his inability to contact anyone before, but he was a little taken aback at the sincerity with which Ulysses was now approaching him. Deciding to take him at his word, Dante quickly made contact with John, but only was able to hold it long enough to determine that what Ulysses had told him was apparently true. During the mental connection, Dante felt that John was holding something back, deep in the recesses of his mind, but he didn't have time to determine exactly what it was.

"Satisfied? Now, let's get down to business," Ulysses leaned against the control panel. "Please, make yourself comfortable. If you still want to carry through with your mission when I'm finished, you may attempted to do so."

"I'll listen, but I'm going to stay right here and keep holding onto these, regardless. Go ahead," Dante replied.

"Very well," Ulysses said. "I assume you've been told that father and his fellow astronaut were taken captive, poked, prodded, and bared witness to various invasions and sinister activities by the aliens you've recently come into contact with yourself. While I won't deny some of that is true, or else neither of us would be standing here right now, there is a lot you don't know. You see, father's mission was to test the warp drive, but once they made contact with the aliens, the Krockthar race, if you prefer, he was able to radio back to John Dawson for further instructions. You see, the Krockthar were a peaceful race, completely content to study and learn about the universe, only making direct contact with other life forms when unavoidable."

"If they were truly peaceful, then explain how Greta . . ." Dante stopped, feeling a pounding in his head momentarily.

"I said peaceful, not perfect. Please don't interrupt again. I believe I'm being more than fair to you," Ulysses said. "As I was about to say, father attempted to sabotage their ship, and only then did the Krockthar take such definitive measures. They warned father never to return, and were able to sabotage the warp drive, so that it only worked one more time. As for future drives, well, I took care of that . . . with a little help. You see, as I grew more experienced, though my age stayed the same, I was able to exert my influence farther and farther. However, the point is, these creatures were only violent once forced, and as I learned of the treachery lurking in the mind of John Dawson, I simply forced them. You may ask your question."

Dante almost didn't, even though he'd been given "permission." He wasn't scared to ask, but he hated to play into whatever game Ulysses was playing.

"What treachery?"

"John Dawson had every intention of working around father's instructions and attempted several times to build new warp drives and even teleportation devices to find and destroy the Krockthar," Ulysses said. "While it is true that father, through great duress, was convinced you could possibly be the earth's 'only hope' someday, John Dawson had no intention of allowing you to return alive. You'll find that your EMP device works as promised. It will truly knock out our controls long enough for you to set off the other bomb. However, the other bomb's timer will mysteriously fail, and you'll be forced to sacrifice yourself to save mankind. Even with my invasion force already on earth, they will eventually be overcome, with no chance for reinforcements or retreat. You see, John Dawson doesn't believe in allowing the human race to be tainted. Why . . . I believe you may have left behind some hint of your DNA, didn't you? I wonder what John Dawson will do . . ."

Dante was stunned. There was no indication that Ulysses was lying, but Dante was smart enough to know that the truth was somewhere in between his tale and that of John and his father. Even so, he had no doubt that what Ulysses had said about the bombs would prove to be true. Perhaps given time, Dante would be able to find a way to work around that, but he wasn't sure how much time he had left. Dropping the bag gently to the ground, Dante hoped that Ulysses would feel confident enough to stay away from the control panel before Dante could carry through on his new plan.

"I believe you," Dante said, lowering his head.

Ulysses sighed heavily, "Oh, Dante, I'd so hoped we'd be able to avoid this. Do you truly believe I'm unable to read you? Perhaps you'll find comfort in knowing that you won't be the only one to die for a futile cause today, brother."

Dante raised his sword in the air and ran towards Ulysses, but was unable to reach him before he hit another button on the control panel. With one seemingly instant series of motions, Dante's sword repeatedly sliced through the air towards Ulysses, as he matched each swing with an easy dodge.

"Really, Dante, I'm disappointed in you," Ulysses said, reaching behind the panel and grabbing a sword of his own. "Did you actually think that I didn't know what father's plan was? I gave him the plan . . . the sword . . . everything, just to bring you here."

Ulysses shoved Dante back and stepped away from the alien and the control panel.

"Since we do still share much of the same DNA, I'll give you a chance to renounce the human race and rule with me. Think about it, Dante. The invasion has already begun. You would only have to stand by my side and wait as the inevitable occurs. Surely you don't still think you have a chance of victory. They sent you here on a suicide mission. One man against an entire race of aliens. To them, you're just cannon fodder. Stand by my side and be a king, or stand by theirs and die humiliated. It's your choice."

"If you're so powerful, then you already know my answer," Dante said. "You will not win this day. You will not take over Earth. If I fall, then someone will rise and take my place. We have fought through tough times before. We have been told that the cause is hopeless before. Well, Ulysses, the cause is never hopeless. I may indeed die today, but I swear that you won't live to gloat."

Dante ripped off the tattered remains of his Reds jersey and stepped closer to Ulysses, holding his sword out in front with both hands. Ulysses smiled and took the first swing. Dante easily blocked the opening move and returned with a blow of his own. The swords were nearly exact, and each time they connected sparks flew and a nearly deafening clang emerged. Neither man noticed, though, as any loss of concentration would ultimately prove fatal. For what could have been minutes or hours, Dante and Ulysses matched each other moves, swing for swing, with neither man gaining a definite advantage.

Realizing that this could go on for much more time than he could afford, Dante tried to out-think his opponent, rather than out-fight him. He waited for the right moment, when Ulysses was on the offensive, and allowed Ulysses' powerful swing to connect. In the same motion, he dropped to his back and kicked Ulysses' feet out from under him. Ulysses fell with a heavy thud, but Dante knew his alien "brother" was down but not necessarily out. He leapt up from the ground, as Ulysses did the same, and with a spinning move in the air, came down with as much force as he could bring forth, knocking Ulysses sword from his grasp. Ulysses' expression of confidence quickly faded into a look of anger. Keeping on the offensive, Dante used his free hand to punch Ulysses in the jaw, knocking him once more to the ground. He kicked the sword out of his visible range and steadily held his own sword across Ulysses' throat.

"You can't kill me. You won't." Ulysses spoke with a shaky voice, now void of the element of confidence. "We are brothers, Dante. I'm your last connection to father."

Dante removed his foot from Ulysses chest and allowed him to stand, however still keeping his sword across his throat.

"I don't intend to kill you. First, you're going to call off the invasion and bring all the aliens back aboard the ship, and then you're going to teleport back to Earth with me and face up to everything you've done." Dante removed his sword from Ulysses' throat, and instead held it with the point into Ulysses' back as he led him to the control panel.

"Very well. You won fairly, and I am subject to whatever terms of surrender you devise." Ulysses walked slowly with his head down, and his eyes focusing just behind the control panel. "I understand how upset you must be. You obviously are afraid that something will happen to your dear friend or your loving wife."

"Just bring the aliens back and stop talking." Dante paused for a second. "You keep pointing out how we share DNA, how we're family. If you do understand anything about family, then you know that I will kill you if I have to, and figure out how to work everything on my own."

"Yes, I do understand family. I understand that I was left behind by a father I never knew. If he truly cared, he could have found a way to take me with him. This race of aliens wouldn't have lifted a finger to stop him. Even with his betrayal, they would have been content to let all contact end there."

For just a second, Dante lowered his sword and considered what Ulysses had said, which was enough time for Ulysses to reach his hand behind the control panel and point a laser weapon at Dante. He didn't give Dante a chance of reacting as he pulled the trigger and laughed as the resulting blast sent Dante across the room and slammed him into a wall. Ulysses confidently strode across the room, grabbed his sword and then stood over Dante's body, smiling.

"I gave you the choice, Dante. It didn't have to end this way. I honestly would have allowed you to rule with me . . . well, perhaps just beneath me."

Ulysses laughter was cut short as Dante opened his eyes and rammed his sword through Ulysses' abdomen. Dante held firm to the sword as he stood up, and then, after slowly removing the sword and allowing Ulysses to fall to his knees, brought it back for another swing.

"This . . . this isn't the end . . ." Ulysses said, blood gurgling out of his mouth.

"It may not be," Dante said. "But it's yours."

Dante brought the sword down across Ulysses' throat, completely decapitating him. He removed the alien wristband he had taken earlier. Apparently there was a limit to what its power could do. Dante was thankful that it had not shorted out until after he had needed it. Dante paused for a moment standing over his brother's body. He shook his head slowly, feeling a sense of sadness over what could have been and what never was. Throwing those thoughts aside, Dante walked towards the teleportation device and control panel and realized it was nearly an exact duplicate of the one he'd used on earth. Racing to the duffle bag, he reached out mentally to contact John.

"John, can you hear me? Where's Gwen? What happened down there?"

Dante paused a moment, allowing John a chance to deal with another person's voice inside his head. Whether or not it had happened before, Dante knew from experience it was still quite a shock. It was clear that John was seriously injured and still in the midst of fighting, though Dante couldn't tell from his thoughts which side was currently winning.

"I'm . . . I'll be fine with some medical attention, son. We've managed to keep them confined to the lower levels of the base, but it took a great deal of sacrifice. Gwen's safe, though. You'll still be a father." John paused for a moment. "What happened on your end, Dante? We're counting on you."

"Things are being taken care of up here. It took a lot out of me, but I'm still alive, and my 'brother' Ulysses is dead." Dante scanned the ship before continuing. "But there's something I want to . . . I need to know. Before I killed him, Ulysses told me that everything I've been told is a lie. He said that my father was part of a secret mission to attack the planet, and the aliens are only attacking Earth as revenge. Who's telling the truth? Before you answer, remember that I cannot only speak through your mind, but I can also read your thoughts if I have to."

John went silent for a moment, and Dante could see him slowly limp into a small, unmanned room.

"Dante, it's not important. It's over. Carry through with the mission, and we'll discuss everything when you get here. I will answer everything then."

"Rest assured, John, I will come back."

"Dante, you have to understand, it was for the betterment of mankind. I know that doesn't sound like a viable reason to you right now, but you will understand."

Dante broke the connection and pulled out the two metal boxes from the duffle bag, opening each of them and finding everything still intact, as Ulysses had promised. There was a chance he'd be able to scan a few of the scientists and figure out how to fix the timer, but even if he could, there would be no way to be sure they worked if he wasn't still on board the ship. He had no idea how many aliens, if any, were left aboard or if Ulysses had actually messed with the bombs detonation devices somehow. Realizing what he now had to do, Dante made a final connection with Gwen.

"Gwen, I want you to always remember that I love you. I went on this mission for you, and I'm going to finish the mission for you," Dante said, as he opened a one way connection. "It's tearing me up inside that I won't be able to be there for you and our child. I'm not going to give you a chance to respond to this, because I think it would be too easy to talk me out of it. The only way to insure Earth's safety is to blow up the ship, and the only way to make sure that happens is to stay here until the explosions start. I can't . . . I won't be coming home. I have to go now. Please forgive me for leaving you alone. Make sure our child knows who I am, and that I love him, too. I love you, princess. Goodbye."

Dante could feel Gwen's emotions as he finished his message. Her tears became his as he left her mind. He hoped that she would be able to make it through the tough times sure to come with the child, but he couldn't afford to dwell on that now. His resolve was already too weak. He had to finish his mission, and insure that the Krockthar already on earth would have no way to ultimately win. With an image of Gwen planted firmly in his mind's eye, Dante calmly closed the metal box containing the nuke and moved the EMP to the center of the room. Looking around to make sure there would be no surprises, he pressed the button and stepped back. A blast of white, hot light flew through the air, emanating from the EMP, pulsing throughout the ship and beyond. Dante was momentarily deafened and stunned, but he could tell from the lack of power throughout his ship that it had at least worked in the immediate vicinity.

Reaching out to John just enough to determine if there had been any effect on earth, he could see that the Krockthar were a little dazed. Their forcefields still seemed to be working, as they had their own power sources, but somehow they seemed to know that their ships were compromised. That simple realization told Dante that if there were any creatures left on the ship, they'd be able to find him soon. In fact, he could feel them coming, so he quickly raced back to the nuclear device and opened the metal box, closing his eyes and sighing heavily.

Just as he hit the button and in the milliseconds before the device exploded, Dante felt a strange sensation just behind him and the last thing he saw as the nuclear blast ripped through everything in its path was a shimmering, bright light.

EPILOGUE

"DANTE SMITH WAS A HERO, not only to his family, but to the entire human race. He sacrificed his own life, so that we all might live free from the tyranny of an alien race. He will live on in the memories of those of us who were lucky enough to know him, as well as in the hearts of his wife, Gwendolyn, and his newborn son, Dante Conner Smith."

Gwen smiled as John stepped down from the podium, saluting the statue of Dante that had been finally been erected in his honor as part of a memorial gravesite in Arlington National Cemetery. The ceremony was long overdue, but John had insisted they wait until most of the alien invaders had been dealt with. All that remained now were small pockets of resistance, their forcefields long burnt out. It had been nearly a year since she had lost Dante, and, even though the pain was still a large part of her life, the birth of her son had helped to fill the sense of emptiness her husband's death had left. She arose from her seat, handed John the baby, and leaned her head softly against the statue.

"I will always love you, Dante. Nothing can ever change that. Not a day goes by that I don't run to the door everytime the doorbell rings, hoping against hope that it's you. I just want you to know that our son will learn how great his father truly was." As Gwen whispered her words, tears ran down her cheeks. "I forgive you for leaving me alone. I know why you did it. I just wanted . . . I just wanted to say goodbye one last time. I love you."

Gwen reached up and kissed the statue. She wiped the tears from her eyes, gently took her son back from John, and walked quietly out of the cemetery and back to her life. She smiled and kissed her son as she entered the waiting car, feeling Dante's presence and knowing that, somewhere, somehow, he would always be with her, watching over her.

* * *

EPILOGUE 2

It had been nearly a year since Dr. William Grant had moved to Los Angeles from Boston. He loved the weather, or lack thereof, but over that time his cases had grown much stranger. He wasn't sure whether to attribute that to himself, the stereotypes about LA, or just dumb luck, but there was no arguing that the path of his career had taken a definite turn.

"How is our John Doe?" Dr. Grant asked the nurse as he entered the hospital room.

"Still unresponsive, but his burns are nearly completely healed. It's really rather remarkable," she replied.

Dr. Grant nodded his agreement and then looked at the chart for his most recent coma patient. Just a few months ago, someone had brought in a comatose man he claimed to have found in the desert on his way back to LA from Vegas. Although Dr. Grant found the story quite unbelievable, all of the man's alibis had held up and there was no sign of foul play. There was something familiar about the man in a coma, but Dr. Grant couldn't quite place it. *Must be one of those faces, or maybe I just WANT to know who he is.*

"Vitals are steady. There's really no reason he's not conscious," Dr. Grant said, partially to the nurse, partially to himself. "Keep me apprised of the situation. Thank you."

As the nurse smiled and nodded, Dr. Grant took one last look at the patient and then left the room. There would be no answers for him today, but if he continued to play the role he was given then perhaps he would be rewarded with the truth someday.